"Did you do

Gage stared at her over the rim of his wineglass, seducing her with his gaze.

"Yes," Holly breathed.

He offered a sexy smile. "Show me."

"They're in my purse." Holly reached to her left to show him the panties she'd stuffed into her bag.

"No. Show me. Slide your dress up and let me see."

Well, she'd wanted adventure. Holly tugged the material up her legs, past her thighs. The idea of doing this in an upscale restaurant where the waiter could return at any moment was... exciting. Almost as exciting as the heated glint in Gage's dark eyes.

"Are you wet?"

"Yes." Was that really her voice?

"How wet?"

She couldn't take it anymore. Two could play this game. Opening her legs wider, she nudged his hand with her knee. "Why don't you find out for yourself?" she said innocently.

Dear Reader,

I was thrilled to get a chance to set a love story in what I consider one of the most hauntingly romantic cities in the world, Venice. And, of course, a special city demanded a special hero. Enter Gage Carswell, British agent—tall, dark, sexy and as elegantly sophisticated as Venice itself—who's assigned to stop an international threat. What kind of heroine finds herself in Venice? Enter Holly Smith, a rather ordinary schoolteacher from Atlanta, Georgia, in search of her long-lost mother. Stir the pot with a case of mistaken identity and a generous splash of espionage and you've got *Nobody Does It Better*.

While writing this story I laughed, cried and fell in love with a beautiful city all over again, even as I watched Gage and Holly fall in love. I've taken license to create fictional streets, restaurants and businesses just because it's easier that way and as the writer, well, I can. I hope you enjoy the result.

I'd love to hear from you. Drop by my Web site at www.jenniferlabrecque.com to check out my daily blog and www.soapboxqueens.com where Rhonda Nelson, Vicki Lewis Thompson and I blog about this, that and the other.

Happy reading...

Jennifer LaBrecque

NOBODY DOES IT BETTER

Jennifer LaBrecque

TORONTO • NEW YORK • LONDON
AMSTERDAM • PARIS • SYDNEY • HAMBURG
STOCKHOLM • ATHENS • TOKYO • MILAN • MADRID
PRAGUE • WARSAW • BUDAPEST • AUCKLAND

ISBN-13: 978-0-373-79405-8
ISBN-10:   0-373-79405-3

NOBODY DOES IT BETTER

ABOUT THE AUTHOR

After a varied career path that included barbecue-joint waitress, corporate number cruncher and bug-business maven, Jennifer LaBrecque found her true calling writing contemporary romance. Named 2001 Notable New Author of the Year and 2002 winner of the prestigious Maggie Award for Excellence, she is also a two-time RITA® Award finalist. Jennifer lives in suburban Atlanta with her husband, an active daughter, one really bad cat, two precocious greyhounds and a Chihuahua who runs the whole show.

Books by Jennifer LaBrecque

HARLEQUIN BLAZE
206—DARING IN THE DARK
228—ANTICIPATION
262—HIGHLAND FLING
367—THE BIG HEAT

HARLEQUIN TEMPTATION
886—BARELY MISTAKEN
904—BARELY DECENT
952—BARELY BEHAVING
992—BETTER THAN CHOCOLATE
1012—REALLY HOT!

To the guys and gals who show up at the Soapbox
Queens blog (www.soapboxqueens.com).
Y'all are the best

1

"IT LOOKS AS IF WE'LL BE flying with clear skies tonight out of Atlanta and across the pond. We expect to have you in London by 8:00 a.m. tomorrow morning, their time."

Holly Smith relaxed her grip on the armrest. She was flying. Yes, indeed. Maybe she shouldn't have ordered that third glass of wine at the airport bar, but she had a pleasant buzz going and she wouldn't be nearly as relaxed otherwise. So far, flying wasn't as bad as she'd imagined it might be.

Despite what her ex-boyfriend Greg had said, she was not a neurotic mess. So she had some quirks. Who didn't? Who cared if she checked her silverware for cleanliness in a restaurant before she used it, and had brought along her own blow-up travel pillow and blanket so she wouldn't have to use the airline's? And, she was careful with her money. But cheap? She thought not.

A neurotic mess? Hardly. A mess was just ugly. A person couldn't be a mess, spilt milk was a mess. Screw him. She nearly laughed aloud. Nope, she wouldn't be doing that anymore. And hadn't he been surprised to hear it?

She'd known they were in a go-nowhere relationship. Ending that had been the first step in her new plan to make all aspects of her life proactive rather than reactive.

It was rather funny how such a life-changing event had started out so innocuously. Three months ago, she'd been waiting in the hair salon to be called back for a wash and trim. She'd been thumbing through a magazine when she'd stumbled across an article. Usually, she never read those pseudo-self-help pieces, but she'd found herself sucked into this one. The article focused on *being* the change you wanted in your life rather than waiting for someone to change it for you. It had been an aha, scales-falling-from-her-eyes moment.

She took charge in so many other aspects of her life. She'd deliberately pursued a high school teaching career that focused on working with gifted students. She'd set a goal and achieved it. Buying her condo? Same thing.

The "aha" had come in the relationship department. It was as if she'd discovered thousands of dollars of therapy between the covers of one glossy magazine.

She'd realized she was the queen of reactive relationships because…*drumroll*…she didn't trust herself. She'd known she and Greg were going nowhere but she would've waited on him to end it. *Her* breaking up with *him* had been huge. It'd been like getting to base camp on a Mount Everest climb—an important first step.

She reached overhead to direct the stream of cool air from the vent more directly in her face. That felt good. She just wouldn't think about all the germs that were probably in all that recycled air. So far, so good on flying. Of course, they weren't there yet. She exhaled, trying to release the anxiety that suddenly welled up within her. When she got really upset she threw up. And throwing up right now…not good.

"A little nervous about flying?" the woman in the

window seat next to her asked, a note of sympathy in the question.

"Just a little," Holly said. She dug into her backpack and pulled out the inflatable pillow and a small travel blanket. "I've never flown before."

"You picked a long flight for a first timer."

Holly grinned. "Only because the boat takes too long to get from Atlanta to Venice." There was a kernel of truth in her humor. Three quick breaths and the neck pillow was done. She fumbled with the plug for a second, but then got it.

"If you don't mind me asking, I have to know what or who is so important in Venice that you're willing to take such a long first trip?" The woman chuckled. "Sorry. Don't answer that if it's too personal. I'm a writer and I always want to know stuff. My husband says I'm nosy. I consider it research."

"A writer? No kidding?" Wow. "What do you write?"

"I'm Martina Larson. Call me Marty. I write romance novels."

Holly read her fair share of romance novels. Who in the world didn't love a happy ending? The woman's name was vaguely familiar. "I think I've read a couple of your books before. They're very…sensual." If they were the ones she thought they were, they were quite *spicy*. Just the kind of sex she wished she was having. But not trusting herself in a relationship also translated to not trusting herself to indulge in some of her more explicit fantasies.

Marty laughed. "My books go way beyond sensual. I'm on my way to a writers' retreat with a couple of friends. We'll be staying in a sixteenth-century castle a few hours north of London." She paused. "You never said why you're going to Venice."

"I've heard it's beautiful." And that was true.

"It is. And it shouldn't be too crowded at this time of year, at least not as crowded as in the summer. Short of going to the Venetian in Vegas, there's no mistaking Venice for anywhere else. My husband and I spent a couple of days there several years ago."

Had Marty abandoned her family, left behind a husband and two children, and stayed in Venice? Had *she* gone on a business trip and then virtually dropped off the face of the earth? No birthday cards, no Christmas cards, no appearance at high school or college graduation, no contact for twenty-seven years. Holly's wild guess was probably not.

"I want to see it for myself," she said.

"Are you meeting a friend there?"

"No. I'm going solo. But I have arranged for a tour guide, since I have an abysmal sense of direction." This was her mission, her quest, her confrontation. She wanted a firsthand reckoning with the woman who'd birthed her and then abandoned her.

She thought she'd put it behind her, the Mother's Day Tea in kindergarten when the teaching assistant had sat with her because she'd been alone. Being thirteen and having to get up the nerve to approach her father and tell him she needed sanitary napkins. Unlike her friends, she didn't have a mother to prepare her. She'd told herself she couldn't miss what she'd never known. And since Julia, as Holly mentally referred to her, had skipped town when Holly was three, she had no recollection of a time when she'd *had* a mother.

But that wasn't exactly true. Deep inside, for as long as she could remember, she'd been waiting—nurturing a secret hope that one day the phone would ring, a letter would arrive in the mail, that Julia would show up on her doorstep. Her father had finally started to date last year and remarried this year. And Holly had figured it out. Dumping Greg was base camp. Finding Julia was Everest.

"You'll love it," Marty said.

"I think it'll change my life."

Marty eyed her with a mix of speculation and curiosity, as if she knew there was more to the story than Holly was telling. But they were interrupted when the flight attendant announced the upcoming in-flight movie, a romantic comedy.

"Oh, I've been dying to see this. I missed it at the movies," Marty said.

After all the anticipation and anxiety—and probably the wine—exhaustion overwhelmed Holly. She settled the pillow around her neck and unfolded the blanket, tucking it over her shoulders. "If you'll excuse me, I'm going to take a nap. If it looks like we're going to crash, please don't wake me."

She closed her eyes and tried to relax beneath the blanket. She was only partially kidding.

"WE SPOTTED HER ENTERING London under the name Holly Smith." Gage Carswell leaned forward for a better look at the blurry photo enlarged from the airport-security camera as Mason continued his briefing. "She's catching a connector to Venice. We'll delay the flight out of London, which should give you ample time to get in place. We ran her schedule. She's booked a room off of San

Marco for a week. You're going to be in the room next door. She's arranged for a private tour guide, requesting an off-the-beaten-path experience. Your cover will be as that guide. Monitor her twenty-four/seven. We want to know where she goes, whom she sees, what she does. We need contact information. Names. Numbers." Mason shrugged. "Set a honey trap."

Ten years in the spook business and Gage still found all of the spy lingo amusing. Why the hell didn't his handler just say don't kill her, seduce her. He was not, however, amused at being tagged for a honey-trap assignment. Bloody bother, that. He didn't mask his annoyance.

Mason's clipped chuckle lacked any warmth. Sadistic bastard. "I know the seduction routine isn't your preferred MO, but Eros is currently undercover."

The legendary agent Eros who had never met a woman he couldn't seduce to get what—or whom—he wanted. Kazbekistan? Poor sot. At least the food would be better in Venice.

Gage settled back in his chair in the windowless office. Paranoia and caution went with the job of managing covert operations, but it would drive Gage nutters to spend every day in this box, even if it was in London. However, windows meant the other side could use a telephoto lens or other high-tech methods of gleaning information on a desk or computer screen that didn't want gleaning. Give him his field-operative position any day.

He glanced again at the photo of the woman Mason had included in his briefing papers. The Gorgon, aka Holly Smith. Five foot six. Weight listed at one-forty, but Gage figured that contained a fifteen-pound lie. Women couldn't resist shaving down the number. Chin-length brown hair, and startling aquamarine eyes in an otherwise average face. From what he ascertained from the photo, she wasn't a beauty, but she wouldn't set small children off screaming, either.

"Why would she book a tour?" Gage asked. It didn't make sense.

"As a cover?" Mason shrugged. "To be unpredictable? Because she's a bloody female?"

Not for the first time, Gage thought Mason was something of a misogynist, but that wasn't his problem. "There's a tour itinerary?"

Mason flicked his wrist toward the file. "It's in there, as dictated by the client."

"It's a private tour group? Isn't there an office?"

"No. Your Way Tours is an Internet operation touted as being more low-key and personalized than trolling along with the blue-hairs. Consider it your lucky day that you won't have to wear a natty polyester suit coat, too."

"You're sure she's the one?" Gage ran a finger along the edge of the photo. He'd heard of the woman code-named the Gorgon. Dealing in black-market uranium, she'd proven to be an elusive target for years. But they'd been getting closer and closer. It was only a matter of time. One slipup, and they'd have her.

Mason steepled his fingers and regarded Gage across the expanse of desktop separating them, his pale green eyes cold despite his smile. "Holly Smith is either an alias or a stolen identity." He shrugged. "It doesn't matter. It's her." Mason shook his head. "She might as well have a tattoo across her forehead with those aqua eyes. They're unique—her one identifying mark. She could easily mask them with colored contacts but she won't. Female vanity.

True, she's never operated in Venice before, but if it looks like a Gorgon, walks like a Gorgon, smells like a Gorgon…"

"It's a Gorgon," Gage finished for him.

"There's been some chatter indicating a substantial deal impending. With the Gorgon's arrival in Europe, it appears imminent. We could be looking at a drop." Did Mason always have to sound as if he had a stick up his arse? "If so, it's imperative we intercept the package. By the way, you're going in as an illegal. The Italians don't like us poaching on their territory."

"Not a problem." It seemed a bit of overkill for a simple watch-and-monitor situation, but he'd gone in without diplomatic immunity before. If he was caught out, he was on his own.

"Unbeknownst to the ubiquitous Ms. Smith, her travel case has been *misplaced* at Heathrow. Pity that. It didn't manage to make the connecting flight to Venice."

"We've examined it?"

"We will soon enough. If there's a package, we'll find it. Even so, we'll still want contacts. Holly Smith is being monitored now, but once she steps off the plane in Italy, she's yours. You're to initiate contact at 9:00 a.m. at her hotel tomorrow morning. Her tour includes three meals. She specifically requested a Venetian native, a middle-aged female preferred. Her assigned guide, Signora Ciavelli, however, has developed a sudden and most unfortunate gastric problem and you're to be her substitute. You're not a native but you lived there immediately following university."

It'd require finesse to tail the Gorgon from the airport to the hotel. Even a glimpse of him could give away the game. Familiar anticipation surged through him. He looked forward to outfoxing his new opponent.

"Are we tipping our hand with the missing luggage and the suddenly sick guide?"

"We've calculated the risk," Mason assured him. "We couldn't chance the luggage going through. The most obvious place to hide something is right in front of one's nose. And we need you with her constantly. Unfortunately, I'm not convinced your charm is such that you could sweep her off her feet. And if you try and fail to sweep her off her feet, then you'll simply appear to be a nutter. Inserting you as the guide was a safer bet. She'll be stuck with you."

Gage took the insult in stride. Surveillance, not charm, was his forte. "That works."

A brusque nod and Mason continued, "You're the mate of a mate who owns the guide service. Given your flexible schedule as a gallery owner, you help out in a pinch."

One of the first lessons in spook training—stick as close to the truth as possible. One was less likely to trip oneself up when one put forth the least amount of lies. Actually, owning an art gallery was not only financially lucrative for Gage, it also offered him the flexibility to extend the range of his spy activities, chiefly because Agnes, his second in command, was a paragon of efficiency and organization.

It amused Gage that spy novels and films often showed an agent simply rushing about, being an agent, whereas in actuality, a legitimate career offered the perfect cover and a measure of interest between assignments.

"And when I get the information?" It was only a matter of *when,* not *if.* What he lacked in charm, he made up for in determination and skill. He wasn't arrogant, just sure of his capabilities.

And he knew he'd never have to worry about getting personally involved. There was a void inside him, the detachment that was a curse for him as a man but a godsend as a spy. He'd never cultivated the detachment. It'd never been a conscious decision not to let another human being touch him emotionally. It'd simply transpired. He'd lost his parents to an auto accident and been sent to live with a grandfather who wanted nothing to do with a nine-year-old lad in mourning. Within weeks, he'd been shipped off to boarding school. From that time forward, there'd always been a distance inside him that buffered him from everyone else, that kept him slightly removed, apart. It served him well in this business.

"Once you've verified the information, let her go and we'll continue to watch her. Just make sure you're not compromised."

He didn't need the reminder of what being compromised entailed. All operative positions were not created equal. His position demanded anonymity. For him, compromise meant, at worst, termination by the enemy or, at best, "retirement" by his agency.

Gage glanced down at the photo of the woman and tamped back a faint tinge of relief that he didn't have to terminate the Gorgon afterward.

Maybe he was getting soft, but he hated it when that happened.

2

HOLLY STOOD WITH HER FEET braced in the vaporetto, Venice's water bus, and stared ahead at the city etched against a star-scattered backdrop, enchanted by the centuries-old spires and domes that punctuated the skyline. She resisted the urge to pinch herself. She'd finally arrived, albeit several hours late.

Cool air whipped her hair behind her and she tugged her jacket more firmly around her middle. Her entire body tingled, as if caught up in an awakening. It was the oddest thing, but the sensation had started when she'd exited the Venice airport.

"It's almost surreal, isn't it?"

She turned to the young couple at the rail beside her. She'd met them while waiting to clear Italian Customs, much the same as when you struck up a conversation with someone in the grocery line. She knew they were art-history grad students from Boston who'd just married and were honeymooning in Venice, but she didn't know their names. "We're not in Kansas anymore, Toto."

"Was it worth it?" the young woman asked with a smile.

"Probably. When I've had a little distance from this day."

"You've had the trip from hell, haven't you?" the new

husband said with an earnest grimace. "Sitting three hours on the tarmac at Heathrow and then learning that your luggage didn't make it to Venice."

"The trip from hell about sums it up." When Holly had finally figured out her suitcase was a no-show at Venice's Marco Polo Airport, the woman behind the counter assured her it would be delivered to her hotel by early morning. It was frustrating, but if they'd deliver her bag bright and early tomorrow morning, it wouldn't be too bad.

In the interim, Holly had no clean underwear, no clean clothes and no makeup. At least she had her travel toothbrush with her. No toothpaste, mind you, but a toothbrush. Cup half-full, cup half-full, she reminded herself.

She shrugged. "I'm looking on the bright side. The plane didn't crash."

"There's always the trip back," the young man quipped with a laugh.

His new wife elbowed him. "Mark! That's a terrible thing to say." Nonetheless, she giggled and wrapped an adoring arm around his waist.

God, they were so young and so in love. They barely looked older than the sixteen-year-olds that came through Holly's classroom. Or maybe she was just getting old. Mark murmured something low and intimate into his wife's ear and Holly looked away from what had become a private moment between the two.

Had she ever felt that way about anyone? Had she ever gazed at anyone with stars in her eyes? Uh, no. Did she want to? Despite Greg's accusations to the contrary, of course she did, didn't she? Well, not necessarily with stars in her eyes. It felt too much like being blinded, and that certainly wasn't good. Her parents had been blinded and she knew how well that had worked out.

The vaporetto, much larger than many of the smaller craft they'd passed, slowed and navigated toward the landing. Her heart thumped harder in her chest as the boat docked with a slight jar.

Holly was literally awestruck. No travel guide, no video could have prepared her for this. The city was an entity unto itself. Elegant and beautiful with an air of mystery and sadness. Was this how her mother had felt all those years ago? Enchanted? Seduced by a place to the point that a husband and children back home became meaningless? Holly shook her head. That's why she was here. She wanted answers. No more wondering. No more supposition.

She wrapped her fingers around the leather straps of her backpack-like purse. This was her stop. She'd memorized it, worried she'd miss it and wind up taking the scenic tour of Venice via vaporetto because she didn't get off when she should. She considered herself very capable, but she had to admit, her sense of direction left a lot to be desired. It was the running family joke that Holly could get lost going from one room to the other in a two-room house. It wasn't that far off the mark.

In a flurry of activity, several passengers exited the boat to the stone quay and Holly found herself in a momentary crush. Her breath caught in her throat as she gained her footing on the worn, slightly uneven stone. She could be standing in the same spot Marco Polo had once stood, perhaps one of the powerful doges, a beautiful courtesan, or one of the countless servants to the wealthy families that had ruled this city of power and intrigue. Lyrical Italian floated around her and she thought the young family to her left was speaking German, but it was English she heard spoken at her elbow.

"Where's your hotel again?" Mark, the Bostonian newlywed, asked as he retrieved a folded map of Venice from his backpack.

Holly rattled off the address of the modestly priced Pensione Armand. She'd forsaken amenities for price while maintaining a location central to the Grand Canal and San Marco square.

"Our hotel isn't far from yours. Want to walk together?" he said.

Holly knew from their earlier conversation that the couple was scrimping on day-to-day expenses so they could splurge on a gondola ride. Holly had silently suppressed a shudder and kept her opinion to herself. True, the gondola was the quintessential symbol of Venice and purportedly the ultimate romantic experience, but they were welcome to it.

Yuck. God only knew what kind of germs thrived in the Venetian canals. The vaporetto was one thing—there was plenty of boat between her and the water. However, she had no interest in getting in a gondola, which would put her in alarmingly close contact with the water. Thanks, but no thanks. She'd admire the graceful black boats with their attendant striped-shirt gondoliers from a distance.

And if the newlyweds wanted to walk now she was more than happy to go with them. She could have been deposited at her pensione canal-side, but her budget didn't include an expensive water taxi. And on the map, it hadn't looked like a long walk from the vaporetto stop. But she wouldn't mind the company. While she had some neuroses, she'd never been paranoid. However, ever since she'd landed in London, she'd felt as if she was being watched.

"Sure. I'd love to walk."

The three of them set off. Staged lights bathed some of the buildings, gilding them with gold. The streets were busy. Couples strolled by, arm in arm. Outdoor cafés hummed with conversation and music. Holly was surprised by how many people were out, but it made sense considering that Venice was a pedestrian-only city.

Mark and his bride easily kept her pace, and conversation between her and the young couple waned. They had obviously succumbed to the soft spring night in the exotically romantic setting. And judging by the looks passing between them, they were several hormones beyond sightseeing and small talk.

Holly was sure the newlyweds were eager to reach their hotel and get their honeymoon in full swing. Venice was made for lovers. As if punctuating the thought, a man and a woman stood silhouetted, sharing a kiss, on one of the picturesque stone bridges spanning the canal.

A wave of sensual longing washed over her. She missed the company of a man. It would be nice to explore the city with a special someone, to feel the warmth of his fingers at her waist, to meet his promising glance, to steal a kiss and have one stolen beneath the lamplight's glow.

She bit back a sigh. At heart she was a romantic, and those were the things a true romantic yearned for. But life had taught her that being practical and pragmatic took one much further. She knew she was too quick to fall into relationships, and inevitably, she was disappointed.

She pushed aside the faint tingle of awareness and longing that had danced along her skin since clearing customs. An alarming thought came to her and she quickened her pace. Her room. What if it was gone? She was hours late for check-in.

Late. Luggage-less. And hungry. Finding herself roomless would cap a spectacularly draining day.

GAGE TAILED THE THREESOME from a distance. He'd managed to overhear most of the conversation on the vaporetto by positioning himself behind them. And on exiting the craft, he'd brushed against her, planting a nearly nondiscernible audio bug on her knapsack.

Although he had yet to actually see the Gorgon face-to-face, because it'd been crucial she not glimpse him, he could now pick her out of any crowd from a distance. Her distinctive walk combined a straight-forward stride with a sensual slight hip roll.

Gage turned left and followed them down the narrow winding street that branched off of the square, dropping back even farther as pedestrian traffic thinned.

Spy technology had enjoyed some impressive advances since he'd joined the business. Now, even though he was a few hundred meters behind them, he could clearly hear their conversation, that is, were they to actually engage in it.

His listening device replicated one of the hands-free mobile phone devices worn in the ear, but this one was custom-made for him. A couple of years ago, if someone had stolen the device, they would've been able to hear whatever he was hearing. But now, the piece only transmitted from the listening device if it recognized the shape of his ear, which was, in effect, the pass code for the piece to function as a listening device. Otherwise it was simply another mobile phone earpiece.

Bloody brilliant it was. He loved all the *toys* that came with his assignments. Prior to the Gorgon's landing, he'd bugged both her room and the loo with audio and video. Her every move would be recorded. And if anyone were to leave a package in her room in her absence, he'd know. Were she to send or receive a text message, he'd know. Before the week's end, he'd be privy to all of the Gorgon's secrets. One way or another.

They'd almost reached the pensione. Gage darted down an alley shortcut, barely big enough for two, that would put him at the hotel ahead of them. His gut told him the couple wasn't a contact. Gage excelled at discerning body language and coded glances. He'd guess the Gorgon had befriended them as a cover…or perhaps, as a sexual conquest.

Rumor had it that while the Gorgon might look like the girl next door, she had a penchant for a casual ménage a trois now and then. Would she issue an invitation or was she merely initiating contact before the seduction?

"It should be just ahead," the bloke said.

"Thank you, both. It was a pleasure meeting you. Maybe we'll run into one another again?"

"That'd be nice," the woman said. "We're just…what, Mark…two streets over?"

"More like one and a half."

For someone with the Gorgon's skills, tracking them again would prove easy, Gage thought to himself. She'd invite them to meet her for drinks. One, perhaps two, bottles of Valpolicella later, the wife would visit the loo and the Gorgon would make her move.

She'd lean in close and in her honeyed, slightly smoky, Southern tone, she'd ask if he'd ever had two women at once. She'd murmur of the pleasure to be had by two eager mouths to suck, nibble and kiss all around his world, four skillful hands to stroke and knead him, two of *everything* intent on pleasuring him. For one night, wouldn't he like to be the center of attention of two women? No one knew them here. No one would know afterward. It would be their secret pleasure. Maybe she'd slide her hand over his thigh, brush her fingers against his cock, and Mark would convince his bride to play because there wasn't a man alive, despite what he might tell his wife or girlfriend to the contrary, who wouldn't want that.

But that would come later. Now the Gorgon merely shared pleasantries. Gage entered the lobby as the trio turned onto the street and quickly mounted the stairs. It would be interesting to discover what contact she'd make once she gained the privacy of her room.

SHE HAD A ROOM. YAY. One potential disaster averted. Holly couldn't stop smiling as she climbed the wooden stairs behind the proprietress.

It had sounded as if she said her name was Signora Provolone. Holly was certain it was her horrible ear for foreign languages, combined with hunger that had her thinking the woman's surname was a type of cheese.

After putting in hours studying Italian language tapes, Holly could manage. Proficient, however, was a stretch.

She followed Mrs. Cheese up a third flight of stairs. Despite her exhaustion, Holly was pleased with the hotel. Like everything else she'd seen since arriving, it struck her as enchanting and romantic. There was a faint shabbiness in the threadbare upholstery of the chairs in the lobby, but it suited Holly far more than one of the opulent palazzo hotels would have.

Simple, yet clean. She welcomed the underlying antiseptic aroma of cleaner and wood polish. She also appreciated the old-world courtesy of the woman showing her to her room rather than handing off a key and sending her on her merry way.

Using a skeleton key with a room tag hanging off the end, the other woman unlocked the door at the end of the short hallway off of the top of the landing. No encoded door cards at the Pensione Armand. She handed Holly the key and ushered her into her sparsely furnished, immaculate quarters.

The room itself was narrow with tall ceilings. An arched shuttered window stood opposite the door. Ochre plaster walls warmed the space under the glow of a vintage glass-globed bedside lamp. Hanging above the standard double bed with its simple counterpane, was an oil rendering of the Grand Canal choked with gondolas and other craft in a regatta. A small writing table and chair sat next to a chifforobe. No television. No phone. Lovely.

"Bathroom?"

Signora Provolone beamed and indicated the door next to the chifforobe.

While Holly had booked one of the least-expensive hotels, she'd splurged for a room with private facilities. The idea of a communal bathroom hoisted her germaphobe flag.

The woman's fast Italian was lost on Holly, but it was easy enough to follow her to the door tucked in the corner.

Signora opened the door and stepped back. A sink, toilet and an unenclosed shower—showerhead on the wall with drain in the floor, no shower curtain or glass walls— seemed as clean as the rest of the hotel. Holly's relief, however, faded at the door opposite the one she stood in.

"This is a private bathroom, right?" What was the word? *"Solo? Uno?"*

"No, no, no." It didn't take a rocket scientist to figure out from the proprietress's hand gestures that Holly would be sharing the room with another guest. The woman brushed past Holly and explained in heavily accented English with more accompanying gestures. The setup was sort of a Jack-n-Jill deal—her interpretation, not Mrs. Provolone's. When she wanted to use the facility, she was to lock the door leading to the other room from the bathroom. When she was finished and the bathroom was available, she was to unlock the door from inside, close her door behind her and then lock her door from inside her room. Signora Cheese finished her instructions and beamed hopefully at Holly. "Yes?"

Howling in frustration seemed unlikely to get her anywhere other than tossed out. Thank goodness she'd packed a full supply of antiseptic towelettes. Packed. In her luggage. Which wasn't here. Never mind.

She pasted on what she hoped passed for a smile. "Yes. *Grazi.*"

The woman left and Holly stood in the center of the room, rolling her head on her neck slowly to release tension. After nearly thirty hours of traveling, thanks to time changes and flight delays, she welcomed the room's peace and quiet.

She longed for a hot shower, but first things first. She

might be pushing the backside of thirty, but her father and her newly minted stepmother, Marcia, had insisted she call once she was safely ensconced in her hotel room. She and her father had always been close, but her decision to find Julia had strained their relationship, particularly once her father realized he couldn't talk her out of going. Holly thought it was a combination of him not wanting her to get hurt, as well as his feeling as if her determination to find Julia was an insult to him.

She turned on the cell phone reserved for occasional use, thanks to the exorbitant prices per minute charged. Her dad answered on the second ring.

"I'm here. Finally." No need to mention the lost luggage.

"Thank God. Have you talked to your guide yet?"

"No. Not until tomorrow. The flight delay didn't affect that."

"No trouble getting to the hotel?" her father asked.

"I had some help," she admitted, crossing to open the shuttered window and look out onto the curved street. She almost felt as if she were dreaming.

"Be careful." Her father was a little on the overprotective side. Most likely from being a single parent all these years, and the fact that she was the youngest and a girl. He definitely wasn't this way with her brother, Kyle.

"I'm always careful."

"Just remember, you're in a foreign country."

"I'll be extra careful." The conversation felt awkward, but then, things had been awkward for a few weeks now. Her father had nearly come unglued at Holly's decision to find her mother. And when he'd grudgingly confessed that he knew precisely where Julia was because he'd kept up with her whereabouts all these years but never shared the information with her or Kyle, things had definitely been tense.

Actually, *tense* was an understatement. Kyle had been pissed off that Daddy had left them in the dark all this time. Even Sherrie, Kyle's sweet wife, who always gave people the benefit of the doubt, had thought it was a crappy thing for their father to do.

Once Daddy had divulged that Julia was still in Venice after twenty-seven years—and saved Holly a ton of search time—she'd declared her intent to travel to Venice, which yet again polarized the family, this time along gender lines.

Kyle thought her spending the time, money and effort to travel to Venice to find Julia was, as he so charmingly put it, "bullshit." Her father was also dead-set against it.

Her stepmother, however, had supported Holly's decision. Marcia saw it as a means for Holly to balance her heart chakra. Holly wasn't sure she bought into the whole chakra thing, but she appreciated Marcia's support. Sherrie had also thrown her towel into the "Julia meet-'n'-greet" arena, sending school photos of Holly's niece and nephew and a Wal-Mart family portrait of Kyle, Sherrie and the kids for Holly to share with Julia. Even her cousin Josephine, who had been raised by their grandmother after rebel African soldiers killed her missionary parents, and who was often standoffish and prickly, had jumped in to support Holly's decision. Josephine, a veteran traveler, was the one who suggested Your Way Travel, a private tour guide operation, given Venice's winding, confusing streets and Holly's terrible sense of direction.

Holly found it ironic that Julia had ripped their family apart at the seams years ago and was still tearing at their familial fabric even now. It would've been so much easier if Holly had simply abandoned her plans for the sake of maintaining family peace, but scaling this mountain was too important to her.

She had all kinds of conflicting emotions about Julia and what she wanted the outcome of this meeting to be, but in a weird way, the outcome was almost secondary. It was the *doing* that was so important. It was Holly taking a proactive stance and not waiting on the elusive "one day" when her mother might contact her.

"Are you going to see her tomorrow?" her father asked. Maybe if Holly hadn't known him so well, she might've missed the quiet yearning, the silent heartbreak underlying his question. She hoped Marcia was in another room and couldn't hear the same thing Holly did.

"I don't know. I haven't decided yet when I'm going to…" What? March up to her door? Introduce herself as Julia's long-lost daughter, one who'd been deliberately lost? "…initiate contact." Ah, that had a vague, euphemistic feel to it.

"I still think you should call her first."

"I'm not calling." They'd had this discussion countless times, as well. He'd nagged her to call, send a letter, *something* before she hopped on a plane and traveled across the Atlantic. She was equally adamant she wouldn't. Celeste McKinney, one of the teachers at her school, had discovered she was adopted and spent years tracking down her birth mother. She'd called first, to give her mother time to adjust to the idea of meeting her daughter, and the mother had flat-out refused, informing Celeste in no uncertain terms it was best to let sleeping dogs lie. It had crushed Celeste. Holly was determined to face Julia one on one.

She wasn't giving her mother the opportunity to turn her down.

Her father's heavy sigh echoed over the phone. "How about you just call us after you've seen her."

"Fine. Does this time work for you?"

"Whenever you want to call is fine."

She leaned against the window casing and tamped back a flash of homesickness. Venice was beautiful, but home was home. If she'd been home, she'd be in her chair with a book, with Ming curled up on the ottoman. She could do with a little kitty company right about now. And her own nice clean bathroom.

"You're picking up Ming tomorrow?" She'd left her seal-point Siamese rescue at home with plenty of food, water and fresh litter. Dad and Marcia had offered to pick him up and baby-sit him at their house. She knew Marcia was behind the peace offering. "Be careful, he's sneaky. He'll get out if you're not careful."

"We'll take care of him. Don't worry."

"I won't. I'm not buying trouble." The second the words left her mouth she recognized her mistake. She closed the shutters and latched them, propping the cell phone awkwardly between her shoulder and head.

"You bought trouble when you purchased your ticket and got on that plane." Censure marked her father's gruff voice. They'd had this discussion umpteen times since she'd made her decision. She was here and she certainly didn't plan to enter yet another futile argument.

She hurried the call to an end and tossed the cell phone onto the bed. A shower, a good night's sleep and her suitcase should be here tomorrow morning.

Glass half full.

3

THE LOCK CLICKED INTO PLACE on the other side of his door leading to the washroom, and Gage settled back onto the bed in his adjoining room, the laptop monitor giving him a clear view of the loo and the Gorgon's room. The Gorgon proceeded to examine the washroom. She peered into the corners, stood on her tiptoes to check the show-erhead and even gave the toilet itself a cursory once-over.

He grinned and crossed his arms behind his head. He wasn't sure what *she* used in the way of spyware, but Gage employed cutting-edge technology. She could look all day and never detect the motion-activated audio-video equipment planted in both rooms.

She offered an almost imperceptible shrug and leaned into the washroom mirror, peering at her face. A queer feeling jolted through him and he shook it off. Her eyes were positively arresting, yet the rest of her face was sin-gularly unremarkable except for a slightly lush mouth.

She sighed and stepped back. Without ceremony, she unzipped and slipped out of her trousers. He wasn't a voyeur and he would only watch her undress for as long as it took to ascertain she didn't have any information hidden on her.

Her top came past her thighs, but Gage would've had

to be a eunuch—and he wasn't—not to notice and appreciate the lovely length of shapely leg. The Gorgon boasted the legs of a 1940's pinup girl. She neatly folded her trousers and placed them on a towel on the washbasin's edge.

In one fluid motion she tugged the top over her head and all the air seemed to suck right out of Gage's body. Lush rounded curves covered by black knickers, cut high on the thigh and low on the hip, and a black bra. In the center of her chest a small zippered travel pouch was affixed to her two bra straps. Unsnapping the pouch, she stacked it and her top on her trousers.

She raised her arms over her head as she arched her back in a sinuous stretch—a siren's call, all the more difficult not to heed as she was unaware of her audience—and then brought them down and back. She slowly rotated her head on her neck, as if ridding herself of the day's tension, and then rolled her shoulders in an unerringly erotic motion.

She reached between her breasts and unhooked her bra. One simple shrug of her elegantly rounded shoulders and it was gone, joining her trousers and top.

Throughout the years, his gallery had displayed countless art pieces with nude subjects in varying states of undress. Strictly as a chap who appreciated the human form as a work of beauty, he was appreciative. Her back, from neck to hip, was a fluid, sensual work of art. Golden brown nipples tipped full breasts. As a man who hadn't had a lover in months, he noted the alabaster globes, the slight rounding of her belly and the curve of her hips.

She turned and started the shower, stepping aside to avoid the spray. While the water heated, she skimmed her knickers off. A triangle of crisp curls covered the apex between her thighs and her lush bum formed an inverted heart at the base of her spine.

Desire, usually buffered by an emotional distance, slammed into him with a force that shook him. Intense wanting knifed through him, bypassing all rationale and objectivity. She stepped under the shower spray and he deliberately looked away from the screen, drawing a deep breath and holding it before exhaling slowly.

He'd never reacted this way, felt such a…connection to anyone before. His detachment seemed to have deserted him at a most inopportune time.

His operative task was broken down into a series of small objectives, which would ultimately lead to him attaining his primary goal. This particular objective had been satisfied. His cock stirred and he grimaced. *Satisfied* was a piss-poor choice of wording. How about *met?* He'd met his objective. He'd ascertained she wasn't hiding any documents or goods in her clothing, although it could still be in her knapsack or the small pouch she'd worn. To watch her shower moved beyond his professional role and there was no room for that. She was a job. An assignment. Nothing more. Nothing less.

Out of nowhere she moaned, a low, husky direct feed in his ear. Like an adrenaline hit, it shot straight to his cock. What the hell? He glanced at the screen. Her head was tilted back. Water cascaded over her shoulders and the slopes of her honey-tipped breasts, running in rivulets over her belly and down the length of her legs, darkening her pubic hair.

Blood pooled between his thighs, thickening his cock to full attention. So caught up was he in the water flowing over her nakedness, he reached between his legs before he realized what he was about to do.

Bloody hell. He'd never sat about wanking his tool while on assignment and he wasn't about to take it up now. He deliberately looked away, willing his cockstand back down.

He'd go one better than a cold shower. He'd ring Mason with an update.

"Everything's in place?" Mason said. "You had time to set up?"

"Yes. She made contact on her mobile. She says everything is set to proceed as normal tomorrow. She referenced a Ming who's to be picked up tomorrow and she warned he would try to get out."

"We'll see what we can find on a Ming. Any other names? Other references?" Mason's voice sharpened with impatience.

Wouldn't he have said so? Gage merely said, "No. What about her case? Find anything of interest?"

"It's clean. We destroyed it, ripped out the seams in her trousers and knickers, even took the locks apart, nothing. Not that we really expected to find much. Anything of consequence will be on her."

Perhaps in her backpack, or in the pouch she'd carried in her bra but not immediately on her now. The Gorgon was too seasoned to hide anything in her case, although sometimes, the best course of action was the least-anticipated move.

In the next room, the shower stopped. He quickly disconnected the phone.

Listening to the sound of her toweling herself dry, Gage prided himself on his professionalism. There was no need to watch her until she left the washroom. Unfortunately, he seemed singularly incapable of not seeing her in his mind's eye.

Water splashed in the sink and the accompanying sound of her brushing her teeth echoed in his earpiece. The water ran a bit longer and a quick glance at the screen revealed she was rinsing out her knickers, the hotel towel wrapped around her, sarong-style. In short order, she unlocked his door from the inside, indicating it was free for him to use it, exited the washroom and immediately locked her bedroom door behind her.

He watched her via the monitor as she hung her clothes in the wardrobe and her knickers on a hanger to dry. She retrieved a pair of glasses and a small notebook and pen from her knapsack, placing them on the bedside stand.

Gage had monitored other operatives numerous times and always with a clinical detachment. Why then did it feel so intimate to watch her perform these routine tasks?

The Gorgon stood before her bedroom mirror and finger-combed her tangled hair. "My kingdom for a blow dryer," she muttered before turning away in disgust. Gage grinned. Poor Gorgon. But that's what one got when one made a living selling secrets.

She pulled off the towel and draped it over the chair back. "I guess I'll just have to wear the sheet if there's a fire in the middle of the night," she said to her reflection, wrinkling her nose in an innocent way. But Gage knew better. He knew the bad guys weren't always all bad and he knew the good-guy's hats were more often gray than white. Still, it struck him as…well, rather cute. One didn't expect the Gorgon to display a cute side when she was alone in her room talking to herself in the mirror.

That'd get him in for a bloody evaluation in no time. *Yes, Mason, the Gorgon displays a cute side to her when she's alone.* For chrissakes, puppies and kittens were cute, not sodding spooks. Actually, it'd almost be worth it just to watch the look on Mason's face at the thought of his number one agent slipping over the edge.

THE GORGON GASPED HER pleasure. The blond man—was his name Raymond?—tugged harder at her nipple held between his fingers and alternately sucked and nipped at the one in his mouth.

"Do you like that?" Tightening his grip on her massage-oil-slicked thighs, the dark-haired Trevor worked his cock in and out of her harder and faster. She slid her hand up and down Raymond's engorged penis in the same rhythm, scraping her nail lightly against the sensitive ridge on the underside.

Rule one: Don't limit sex to good-looking, well-endowed men. Often the less-attractive ones, or those with smaller dicks, were more grateful and thus much more easily manipulated. They also tried harder to please.

Rule two: She was in charge…and they knew it. No one came until she came.

Rule three: Never let them know her real name or her number. She contacted *them*. It kept it simple and it kept them needy. Even the ones with girlfriends or wives came, no pun intended, when she called. Sometimes, the men even brought their significant others along. She, the Gorgon—she rather liked thinking of herself by that name—had an appetite for things the wives and girlfriends often didn't.

And rule four: Sex was better with three on the playing field.

On the hotel nightstand, her phone vibrated. It'd be *him* with an update. She'd instructed him to text rather than call, telling him she had a meeting. Paranoia, possessiveness and insecurity on his part all worked to her advantage, but he wouldn't like it if he knew what she was doing now.

"Hold that thought, gentlemen," she said, unhanding Raymond's cock. He was the less gifted of the two in the size department. She had plans for him after the commercial break.

She slid up the four-hundred-thread count Egyptian cotton sheets and flipped open her phone. She downloaded the text message and quickly scanned it.

A slow smile curved her mouth and the sexual excitement she'd felt with Raymond and Trevor intensified. Everything in Europe was going precisely as she'd planned. Carswell had been unleashed on the unsuspecting Holly Smith. She flipped her phone closed.

She got off on this spy business. She'd kind of miss it when she retired. She'd have to find something else to occupy her. And this news definitely called for a celebration.

She rolled to her knees and turned to Trevor, where he waited at the end of the bed. "I think it's time we switched things around, gentlemen." She crawled the length of the bed on her hands and knees, her breasts swinging free and heavy. Braced on one hand, she wrapped her other hand around Trevor's cock, teasing her tongue along the tip. He quivered in her palm and her smile widened.

She paused to glance over her shoulder at Raymond. "You're invited to the party, too. But use the back door."

Yes, this called for a celebration, indeed.

GAGE LOUNGED ABOUT IN his bed the following morning, content to do nothing. A bit of a lie-in had always been one of his guilty pleasures. His hard-ass grandfather, the Colonel, had considered it heretical and it hadn't gone over well at boarding school, either.

Better still if it was a lazy rainy day and he had a spot of feminine company between the sheets.

He stretched and bunched the pillow beneath his head. It wasn't as if he could do anything until the Gorgon made a move. Thus far, she'd made an early-morning visit to the loo, which he'd *not* watched once he ascertained there was nothing in her hands.

She nabbed her mobile and dialed, hugging one naked arm around her naked waist right below her naked breasts. Why didn't she put on some bloody clothes? All that nakedness was damned distracting. Naked was a good look on her.

"Buon giorno." She identified herself and gave her room number. "Has my suitcase arrived?" She paused. "You're sure? Thank you. *Grazie.*"

She disconnected the call with a snap of her mobile. "Damn it to hell."

She revisited the wardrobe, feeling her knickers, obviously far from dry judging by her grimace. She sniffed delicately at yesterday's clothes and recoiled. "That's just gross."

Note to self. The Gorgon wasn't a morning person. And she also had the most delicious voice, dropping sharp consonants and rounding itself around vowels, lengthening them in a Southern drawl. He'd never considered himself much of an auditory person, but her voice sent a rush through him. Christ, she even made swearing sound sexy. Not a far stretch at all to imagine her in her lovely naked state whispering a bit of naughtiness in his ear…

She rooted around in her knapsack and punched in a series of numbers on her mobile phone.

In all the spy films, the phone was always being monitored and recorded. But until he found a private moment with her mobile, he was privy only to her end of the conversation.

She identified herself and her flight number to someone on the other end. Ah, she was following up with the airline. He settled back against his pillow. This should prove entertaining.

"My luggage didn't make the flight from London to Venice yesterday. It was supposed to be delivered to my hotel this morning. What? There's no trace of it?" Her voice escalated a notch. "How can you have lost it? It was checked through in Atlanta. I was assured it would be sent to my hotel. Yes, I understand you can't send it if you can't find it. But how about you understand this—*I need underwear!*"

Well, now that she'd destroyed Gage's hearing in that ear… "I washed out my lone pair last night and they haven't dried. I don't want to wear wet panties."

She might be the enemy, but she was magnificent when riled. Her aqua eyes flashed like a stormy sea and her breasts quivered. For chrissake, where was his bloody detachment that had served him so well all his life?

"Does that sound like a good vacation to you? It doesn't to me. Listen, if I didn't want to wear underwear, I would've left them at home in the first place. I don't appreciate your attitude. What's your supervisor's name?

Maybe they can introduce you to the concept of customer service."

Gage took satisfaction in the fact that her missing case had inconvenienced the Gorgon. One had to relish the small victories as they arose.

She disconnected the call. Gage noted the time. Quarter past eight. Grinning, he shoved back the covers and strolled into the washroom, clicking the lock on her door and locking her out of the washroom.

"Crap," she muttered in his ear—well, his earpiece—but it might as well've been in his ear.

His grin broadened and he turned on the shower.

"Ugh. Yuck."

Apparently she'd elected to wear the wet knickers. He pushed the sexual connotation out of his mind. Ah, the Gorgon was going to be in rare form when he met her this morning. Might as well go for broke.

A passable tenor, Gage's voice always improved with the acoustics of a tiled washroom. He burst into a shower rendition of *La Bohéme,* from act one.

"I have descended into the bowels of hell," the Gorgon's voice muttered in his ear.

Gage sang louder.

HOLLY HAD BEEN DETERMINED to put her bad-day karma behind her yesterday…until she'd rolled out of bed naked this morning and discovered still-damp panties, no luggage and a rude airline-customer-service representative.

The only good thing to come of that conversation? She knew her luggage wasn't showing up today. The woman on the phone had actually seemed delighted to tell her if it hadn't arrived by now, it wouldn't make it today.

In the next room, the shower and the singing stopped. Thank God. The voice wasn't particularly unpleasant, but she wasn't in the mood to be serenaded this morning. Yet another grand reason for having requested a private bathroom.

Missing luggage necessitated a change of itinerary. She was more thankful than ever that she'd arranged a private tour guide. She'd specifically requested a woman, slightly older than herself and a Venetian native. Holly would feel comfortable with a woman and she'd look less like a tourist, gaining insight into what it was like to live in Venice. She'd been introduced, via the Internet, to her assigned guide, Signora Ciavelli. Forty-seven, with a slightly round face and dark hair sprinkled with a bit of gray, she'd looked kind and capable in her photo.

Signora Ciavelli would know exactly where they should shop. And shop they would, because clammy panties, clothes she'd worn for thirty-six hours, no makeup and no hair-care products just weren't working for Holly.

She checked out her reflection in the bedroom mirror. To quote her brother, Kyle, she looked like *shit on a stick*. Some women fared well going au naturel. She wasn't one of them.

She knew she wasn't a head-turner. She was just an average woman with odd-colored eyes. The entire time she was growing up, she'd loathed having the eyes she'd inherited from her father's grandmother. She'd hated it when people commented on them because the compliments always ended a little flat, as if it was a pity the rest of her didn't match up. She'd embraced her averageness to the point that when she'd begun earning her own money, she'd started wearing brown-tinted contacts. In fact, she'd had brown eyes for more than a decade. Her mother was the beauty. Thank goodness Holly looked more like her father. She didn't want to be like Julia, flighty and vain. But with all her recent activities, she'd also realized hiding her eye color wasn't exactly embracing who and what she was. Holly had forsaken her contacts several months ago. People still commented on her eyes, but oddly enough, it no longer bothered her. Funny how self-acceptance colored one's perceptions. But there was no coloring her appearance anything but lacking this morning.

She desperately needed concealer for the lovely dark shadows beneath her eyes. As for her hair… She leaned forward and tried fluffing it with her fingers while she held her head upside down. She stood upright again and it looked decent…for about three seconds until it settled back into flat waves against her head. Not a good look.

She'd planned to show up at Julia's address this afternoon. Holly wasn't the great American beauty, but she'd be damned if she'd arrive looking like something the cat had dragged in.

The lock on the other side of her door clicked, signaling the bathroom was available. She might not have toothpaste, but she could at least brush and rinse with water before she ran downstairs.

She stepped into the bathroom, ribbons of steam hanging in the room. She had to admit she liked the scent of the shampoo and cologne lingering in the room. However, the guy must be near-ancient and hard of hearing, considering how loudly he sang in the shower.

She locked the door on his side. Granted, she was only

brushing her teeth, but she still didn't want the old fellow to get confused and wander in.

Five minutes later, she shrugged into her backpack and headed downstairs to meet Signora Ciavelli, determined to turn a bad start into a good day.

She descended the last stairs into the small lobby area, catching a tantalizing whiff of coffee and fresh bread. Holly's stomach growled in recognition. Maybe the scent was wafting in from a kitchen that was out of sight. Maybe it was from somewhere else. She just knew she was hungry. Many pensiones included a continental breakfast but once again, she'd thought to shave a couple of dollars by choosing one that didn't. Besides, her meals were included in her tour.

She'd kill for a cup of coffee and one of the Italian pastries she'd read about in the guidebooks. As soon as Signora Ciavelli showed up, she'd talk her into grabbing a bite to eat.

A couple stood by the front door studying a map and speaking in German…or was it Swiss? Heck, it could've been Russian. She just knew it wasn't English, Italian or French. Tucked in one corner of the room, to the left of the stairs, two chairs upholstered in worn burgundy velvet flanked a small table. A man sat in one chair, his face obscured by a newspaper. The other chair stood unoccupied.

Mrs. Cheese stood behind the dark wood counter that served as the reception desk to the right of the stairs, speaking, in rapid-fire Italian, into a phone propped between her ear and shoulder.

No one, however, remotely resembled Signora Ciavelli. She stepped over to the window beside the heavy wooden door to peer outside. She experienced that same tingling awareness she'd felt the night before when she'd landed at the Marco Polo airport. Maybe it was something in the air here.

"Ms. Smith?"

Startled at hearing her name spoken in a masculine British voice, she whirled around…and found herself in heart-pounding close proximity to one of the sexiest men she'd ever encountered. Average height, dark hair worn a little longish, a lean jaw, dark eyes rimmed in thick dark lashes beneath heavy eyebrows and a hard, masculine mouth. "Yes. And you are…?"

Don't let it be Signora Ciavelli with a sex change, which wasn't as far-fetched as it might sound, considering her luck the past couple of days.

"Gage Carswell." He thrust a very capable-looking hand with well-shaped fingers toward her. Because she wasn't sure exactly why she shouldn't, she shook hands with the man, whoever he was. His handshake was strong and firm without being a vice grip, and if she thought she'd tingled before… His touch resonated through her, all the way to her toes. "Signora Ciavelli had a medical emergency. She'll be fine, but I'll be taking her place this week."

She'd never met him before, she was sure of it. But something about him teased at her, a familiarity she couldn't quite identify.

"But you're a man." She realized how idiotic her comment sounded the moment it left her mouth.

"I've had occasion to notice." His eyes crinkled at the corners when he smiled, which further upped his make-her-heart-race quota.

"But I requested a woman. And a native." She wanted Signora Ciavelli because they would blend in with the locals and Holly could feel relaxed around her. Gage Carswell didn't appear to fit either criteria.

"So I understand. But I lived in Venice for a few years and I'm quite fluent in Italian." To illustrate his point, he broke into the language. She *thought* he said he looked forward to showing her the beauty of Venice. But he could've said her butt was too wide and her hair disgustingly flat and she wouldn't have known the difference.

The missing piece, however, clicked into place for her. He didn't *look* familiar but he *smelled* familiar. And once he spoke Italian, she placed his voice.

The voice in the shower this morning, the scent that lingered in the steamy room. "You wouldn't happen to be staying here at the hotel, would you?"

"I am. As luck would have it, the room next to yours was available and the agency put me in there." She'd pegged her bathroom buddy as elderly and deaf. When she was wrong, she was really wrong. She didn't want to think about him naked in the bathroom, but her mind seemed intent on painting just that picture for her—wet dark hair, water clinging to well-formed shoulders, white towel knotted low on his hips…

She nodded and worried her lower lip between her teeth. "I recognized your voice when you spoke Italian."

He flashed a not-quite-contrite grin that set off butterflies in her tummy. "The singing this morning. Pardon that. I tend to get carried away."

She was flexible. She could roll with the punches. She was not, however, this flexible. Gage Carswell was too male, too sexy…too everything. He just wouldn't do. "Isn't there someone else they can send for the week?"

"Was my singing that bad?" Another smile and that

tingling blossomed into something that felt dangerously akin to lust.

She did not want to be charmed by him. She didn't need the distraction. And he definitely wasn't part of her plan.

She ignored his comment and his smile. "I wanted a Venetian native."

"And I'm quite sorry that you have to make do with me. The agency has authorized me to refund half of what you paid in recompense."

Well, this was a fine mess. She'd be hopeless navigating her own way around. And now she also had to spend money she hadn't planned to spend to replace her luggage and clothes. If she settled for this guy, she got half of her money back. And being on a tight budget...

"Okay." She just couldn't muster being gracious.

His own smile seemed a tad tight. "So, according to what you'd arranged through the agency, we'll have a spot of breakfast and then it's off to Dorsoduro."

That had been her plan, to check out the southwestern district, or sestiere, which was her mother's last-known address. From what she'd read, it was an area of quiet neighborhoods and charming canals replete with tree-shaded squares, home to wealthy Venetians and foreigners. The Dorsoduro, however, would have to wait until this afternoon.

"There's a change of plans, Mr. Carswell. After breakfast, we're going shopping."

"Want to get the souvenirs out of the way up front?"

She knew her smile was grim. "No. We're going to buy panties."

4

HE'D UNDERGONE EXTENSIVE training in hand-to-hand combat, weaponry and guerrilla warfare tactics. He held a third-degree black belt and the powers-that-be considered him an expert in electronic surveillance. So it was ridiculous that one simple handshake and exchange with this woman had rattled his cage.

Still, one touch and the Gorgon had neatly thrown him for a loop, landing him on his figurative arse. No one had managed to put Gage Carswell in that situation since that first miserable week at boarding school when he'd been literally arse-ended into a rubbish bin by Geoff Winkley and his bully mates. Gage had sworn then and there he'd never find himself in that state again. Although this was figurative rather than literal, it was the same out-of-control feeling. He didn't like it any better this time around.

She turned those brilliant aquamarine eyes on him and a spark kindled low in his belly. "Actually, I'm sure shopping for women's underwear is more than you signed up for as a tour guide." She shook her head and did a good job of looking chagrined, apologetic and annoyed all at once. "The airline lost my luggage, but there's no reason both of us should be punished. If you can point me in the direction of a woman's clothing store, I'll manage. Just consider this morning a freebie and I'll meet you back here, say around one?"

Light slanted through the window in the pensione lobby, tipping her brown lashes with gold. He wasn't quite sure at all why she elicited such a response in him. Aside from her eyes, she possessed a quite ordinary face as he'd already noted.

A creamy complexion with a sprinkling of freckles across her nose, which was a bit longish, a mouth that was at close inspection full and plump, all set within an oval-shaped face. Average height—not gamine enough for cute, not tall and thin enough to merit striking, she looked like a nice young woman. Looks however, could be deceiving and, in her case, deadly, if one relaxed their guard.

Did she suspect he was a plant? She'd certainly been hacked to find him taking Signora Ciavelli's place. Did she need the time alone to alert her contact of the companion change? None of it really mattered because she wasn't going anywhere without him.

He summoned a smile. "Shopping in Venice is never a punishment. My agency would be most unhappy if I left you to your own devices." That was an effing understatement.

"But I'll tell them—"

"If you go alone, I'll simply have to follow at a distance to ensure you don't get lost. I'm charged with your well-being here, and at YWI, we take that very seriously. Leaving you to wander about on your own could get me fired." Surprisingly, that swayed her. He read it in her eyes the instant she decided it wasn't worth the argument. He took her by her arm—once again feeling the energy swirling between them, through him—and steered her toward the door. "Let's have a bite to eat and then we'll go shopping."

"I'm ready for breakfast, but I'd like to check here afterward in case my luggage shows up. I'd rather not waste my time shopping if I don't have to."

"How's your Italian?" He didn't think she'd understood a word he'd said earlier.

"Dismal." She smiled and it literally transformed her face to something quite lovely. "I can *ask* where the bathroom is, but there's no guarantee I'll be able to follow directions unless the person I talk to points."

"Which is why you were very wise to hire a guide. I'll give the desk my mobile phone number. They can ring through if your case arrives."

Gage approached the small counter nestled in an alcove to the right of the front door. The same older woman with slightly graying hair who had shown him to his room yesterday evening sat folding a mountain of washroom linens.

He exchanged greetings with her and explained Ms. Smith was waiting on an important package to be delivered. He then relayed his mobile number as a contact.

The entire time he could feel the Gorgon behind him. He sensed her gaze roaming over him as surely as if she were touching him.

"Everything taken care of?" the Gorgon asked.

"They'll call if your case shows up."

And if a note or any other package was delivered instead, he'd know. He had the Gorgon under control.

"How's your coffee, Ms. Smith?"

A shiver slid down her spine. The timbre of his voice

and that accent was a heady combination to her. Honestly, she could just prop her chin in her hand and listen to him talk, but then she'd look like a total idiot.

"The coffee's excellent." She raised the cup and blew a cooling breath over the surface. She'd surreptitiously examined the china and found it clean and spot-free. She sipped again at the rich, full-bodied brew. It was stronger, more intense, than the coffee she normally drank, but if she'd wanted what she was used to, she would've stayed home. "I'm feeling much more human. Amazing what a little caffeine can do for a person. And it's Holly. Ms. Smith makes you sound like one of my students."

And Holly was almost certain she couldn't teach this man anything he didn't already know. He wore an air of experience and sangfroid as casually as he wore his black slacks and dark brown shirt. She found him one part intimidating, one part intriguing.

"Very well, Holly." The way her name rolled off his tongue shot a small thrill through her. "And I'm Gage. Never underestimate the power of caffeine and food."

Yeah. And panties that weren't clammy against her skin would also go a long way toward making her feel human again. But she wasn't sharing that with a guide who scored an eleven on the one-to-ten hot meter. "There is that. How's yours?"

She'd been torn between the *sfogliatelli,* a ricotta-and-fruit-filled pastry, or a simple brioche. Mr. Carswell—um, Gage—had ordered the brioche and she'd opted for the *sfogliatelli.* She'd lost twelve pounds before the trip, thanks to Weight Watchers, but she'd be damned if she'd count points in Venice. At least the cheese was a protein and there was some fruit in there. Besides, dinner last night had consisted of a hastily scarfed-down granola bar. One bite of the *sfogliatelli* and she'd thought she was in heaven. But then nothing had ever smelled quite as good as the aromas that had assaulted them when they'd walked through the door of the cozy shop with its glass counter of fresh pastries and strong coffee perfuming the air.

"Excellent. The food and drink is outstanding in Venice."

Well, this was some scintillating conversation between. What was next? The weather. She took another bite of *sfogliatelli* and a silence settled between them. Around them, the other patrons chatted in a mix of languages. She heard a snippet or two of English.

When they came in, Holly had snagged a table at the picture window overlooking the narrow stone-paved street.

Holly people-watched through the glass now, a part of her scanning the face of every female passerby on the off chance it might be Julia. That was crazy. Maybe the whole trip was crazy. Doubts crowded her. All the money, the time, the plane trip to find a woman who most likely didn't want to be found. She shook the doubt off. Coming here, finding her mother, meant Holly was taking charge, setting the course of this relationship.

And Holly had been three the last time she'd seen Julia. How likely was she to recognize a woman she hadn't seen since? How likely was it that her mother would stroll by the very café Holly was sitting at on her first full day in Venice? Not likely at all, but she couldn't seem to stop searching the faces for her, all the same.

It was even less likely that her mother would walk into this place, but she still took note of every woman coming in. And if she was honest, it also helped her ignore the heavy thumping of her heart brought on by her substitute tour guide.

He made her…*nervous* wasn't the word. Aware? That was more accurate. Everything about him registered intensely with her—the scent that clung to him, the timbre of his voice, the way his hair curled over his collar, the nearness of his arm and leg to hers, the light touch of his hand to her shoulder as he'd pulled out her chair for her in a very gallant gesture. This was the pits. It had been what? Maybe half an hour, and one look, one touch and she was in hyper-hormonal warp mode. This did not happen to her. Ever. And this was a heck of a time to have it start now.

Perhaps it was the lushness of the city itself, the stage setting, if you will.

But for all she knew, he had a wife and kids waiting in England. At the least, he'd have a girlfriend, possibly a few, back home or scattered throughout Europe. It was her experience, in her cumulative thirty years, if a man that looked like Gage Carswell wasn't attached in some way, shape or form, then he was probably seriously flawed. The good ones got snapped up fast. That was her only explanation, because honest to Pete, just when she thought she'd found a guy who was worth keeping, things headed south. So, while Gage was sexy as sin, chances were he was already taken.

She popped another bite of the pastry in her mouth and chewed slowly. She'd ask him. After all, if Signora Ciavelli had shown up, Holly wouldn't hesitate to inquire about the woman's family. She'd treat Gage Carswell exactly as if he were Signora Ciavelli. She swallowed and reached for her coffee.

"So—"

"What—"

They spoke at the same time.

"Go ahead."

"Go ahead."

Holly laughed and it dispelled some of the awkwardness.

"Please, ladies first."

"How long have you been doing this?"

"I've worked with YWI off and on for several years. I mostly fill in for last-minute emergencies or unexpected bookings, as I'm doing now." He smiled and Holly felt the impact of that simple quirk of his mouth all the way through her. "Travel's a favorite hobby of mine and my schedule is flexible. It works out well. I've covered a lot of the globe. And you? Is this your first trip to Venice?"

"Yes." She didn't mention she'd never been on a plane before, either. He obviously jet-setted around the world. There was no need to look like a total rube. "I'm curious. What do you do that allows you to pack up and leave at a moment's notice?"

"Obviously I'm not a brain surgeon or a route driver." Holly instinctively returned his disarming grin. "I own an art gallery in London. Luckily, my second-in-command is most efficient. Without Agnes, I couldn't come and go as I pleased." His eyes were a dark, nearly impenetrable, black, she noted. "But it works out well. Without boasting, our gallery has presented some amazing new talent in the past decade. Surprising what one can discover with the right contacts."

"I'm sure." She wasn't sure at all. He obviously moved in very different circles than she did. Her biggest discovery through making the right contacts had been that two of her students' parents were part of a wife-swapping club in the Atlanta suburbs. Somehow she didn't think that was what he meant.

"And you're a schoolteacher? What do you teach?"

How'd he…? Oh, yeah, the form she'd filled out for the guide service via the Internet. Catering to individual client interests was what set the agency apart from one of the bigger outfits specializing in preset schedules. She'd listed her basic information, profession and her destination interests on the information sheet e-mailed to her. Everything had been very efficiently handled via the Internet.

Holly found great satisfaction in her job, but it sounded boring compared to traveling the world and running an art gallery. Sort of like international modeling compared to running a family farm in Georgia. She'd spare him the details of teaching. "Yes, I'm a teacher. I teach academically gifted fifteen- and sixteen-year-olds who are more interested in learning about one another." She laughed. "This week we're on spring break. It's a vacation for both the faculty and the students."

His dark eyes crinkled at the corners, issuing a slow, sexy, tumble-her-pulse smile. It was difficult to breathe normally when he smiled like that. "You made an excellent travel choice in Venice. I'm here to ensure you enjoy this experience to the utmost, especially now that I know it's your first time. I'll make sure you leave satisfied."

Satisfied. He was about to talk her right into some real satisfaction with his velvety British voice. She squirmed on her wooden seat, a heat, even more delicious than the *sfogliatelli,* sweeping through her. "I'm sure you will."

"Before we start, let's discuss your preferences. What appeals most? Do you prefer going fast, hitting the high points along the way, or are you more interested in going slow with a more thorough exploration?"

"I think a combination of both," she said, proud of how even her voice sounded when she felt so breathless.

Bad Holly, bad. Down, girl. He meant sightseeing, not sex. Maybe it was the city. Romance, sensuality and mystery seemed part and parcel of Venice. Maybe it was his midnight eyes, or the feathering of his dark hair against his collar, the accent, the attraction that pulsed between them…or all of the above? Whatever it was, she couldn't seem to get sex off her mind.

"We could work it that way." He tapped one long, square-tipped finger on the table. Greg, her most recent ex, had almost effeminate hands. They'd always been an "ewww" factor for her. Mr. Carswell, however, had very masculine hands. A faint scar bisected the smattering of dark hair on his right one. She swallowed at the thought of those hands caressing her bare skin.

"We can start with the fast and then if you discover something that really excites you, we can slow it down," he said. "How does that sound? It's all about making this a pleasurable experience for you."

Well, there was *excite* and then there was *excite*. She knew exactly what would make this a *pleasurable* experience for her. She could almost feel that chiseled mouth moving over her skin, along her neck, nibbling at her shoulder, those square-tipped fingers stroking her. That'd be the slow exploration, and as for the fast, hitting the high points…. Good grief, she had never felt so turned on by a man she'd just met, or known for any period of time, for that matter. *Remember the wife or girlfriend,* she reminded herself.

She crossed her legs and her ankle grazed his shin. A burst of heat sizzled up her leg. "Sorry."

"No problem."

Forget warm, tingling, feeling-gloriously-alive body parts—back to the discussion. "Is that how you normally do it?"

"Don't worry about that. Everyone's different. I want you to have it the way you want it."

What she wanted was a big glass of ice water to douse over her head. "I think going with the fast high points to start is a good plan."

She used her fork to cut her *sfogliatelli* into several bite-size pieces and asked, in what she hoped was a very casual tone, "And how does your wife or girlfriend feel about you taking off for these tour-guide stints?"

She shouldn't feel self-conscious about inquiring. He didn't need to know that simply thinking about her touching him, him touching her in anything more than a platonic manner had her all hot and bothered. She wouldn't hesitate to ask Signora Ciavelli how her husband or boyfriend felt about it. But then again, she hadn't just been sitting here imagining Signora Ciavelli's mouth on her....

"Never been married. No current girlfriend."

"What's wrong with you, then? Do you still live with your mother?" The instant the words came out of her mouth, she wished she could suck them back in, but it was too late.

For a second, he just sat there looking faintly shocked, which made it all the more painful.

"I am so sorry. I don't know why… That was rude. I'm sorry. Forget I said it."

A wicked little smile played around his mouth. He slowly shook his head, his dark eyes alight with a cat-and-mouse glimmer. The polite thing for him to do would be to go along with her "forget I said it." But then it would have been more polite for her not to have said it in the first place.

"I can't possibly forget you consider me flawed because I'm unattached," he almost purred. No doubting who was the cat and who was the mouse. He cocked his head to one side as if perplexed. "Most women I meet seem to find it appealing."

She cradled her coffee cup in her hands. Since he was amused rather than offended, she'd play, but she had no intention of being a mouse. They'd play cat to cat. "Since I've already been rude, let me ask how old you are, Mr. Carswell." She sipped at her coffee.

"Gage," he reminded her. "I'm thirty-two. And no, I don't live with my mum." He tossed the ball back to her and she noticed he had a slight dimple in his left cheek when he smiled. "Any other vital statistics required in assessing my defective status, Holly?"

She'd never particularly thought her name sounded remotely sexy, until he said it.

"Not at this time, Gage." She mimicked his earlier head-cocked-to-one-side regard. "In my experience, successful, seriously handsome, articulate men of your age are in high demand. Unmarried ones aren't so unusual, but ones without a girlfriend, or girlfriends, in the picture are rare. It's usually a bad sign—eligible men don't just float around unattached."

"I'm extremely flattered at being considered seriously handsome and articulate."

She felt gloriously, femininely alive sitting in a pictur-esque café in Europe flirting with a handsome foreigner. She smiled and shot him an amused glance. "I'm sure it's not a news flash for you—" his body language reflected self-assurance rather than vanity, an important distinc-tion in her book "—but I'm happy to oblige your ego."

"How do you know I'm successful? Maybe I'm just Eurotrash."

"It's a possibility, but remote. You wouldn't be working for a company with the reputation yours enjoys if you were."

"Interesting deductions. So, if you were to hazard a guess at what's wrong with me…"

"I don't think you're a slob. You appear fairly well dressed."

"Fairly?" He quirked one dark heavy eyebrow in mock offense.

"I'm obviously not a slave to fashion. You could be wearing all designer labels and I wouldn't know the dif-ference."

"I can live with *fairly,* then. And no, I'm not a slob."

"I doubt, however, that you're overly meticulous, because your hair isn't a rigid cut."

"Are you always so observant?"

"Pretty much. It's a survival skill. With what I do, if I didn't pay attention to nuances and details, I'd be dead." He quirked an inquiring eyebrow, a flicker of surprise in his dark eyes. "Those high school kids can be ruthless…."

"Ah. The classroom mob."

"Some days. So, I'm right? You're not a neatnik?"

"Dead on. I'm middle of the road."

She nodded. "I'd say you're a workaholic and you've got secrets."

If she wasn't so used to reading her kids' expressions and watching for subtle shifts, she would've missed the telltale, albeit faint, flicker of acknowledgment and annoyance. But she was, so she didn't. Otherwise, he wore the same amused expression. "And what's your deductive reasoning behind those conclusions?"

"You're successful enough to pick up and leave at relatively short notice. But you leave to work. Your favorite hobby is actually work."

"Impressive. And how does this make me full of secrets?"

"It doesn't. That's totally unrelated."

"I'm all ears." And annoyed, despite his urbane amusement. She'd caught another faint glimmer in those midnight-dark depths.

Something between them shifted, deepened, one step further than light flirtation.

"Your eyes," she said softly, leaning in toward him. "You're a secret keeper."

"Ah. Now I'm not as impressed with your deductive skills." He leaned in, as well, and the rest of the world seemed to disappear, leaving just the two of them caught up in each other. "Everyone has secrets, Holly. I'd wager behind those flawlessly beautiful eyes, you have a few secrets of your own." His dark gaze held her, piercing, probing, and she'd never been so happy that she'd abandoned her brown contacts. "I'd be fascinated to discover what you're hiding behind that girl-next-door exterior." His voice, low and intimate, strummed through her.

She hugged his *flawlessly beautiful eyes* comment to

herself, not feeling as if he found the rest of her dismally lacking. "No. No secrets here." All of a sudden she wasn't so sure. It was as if he was a gatekeeper to a part of her she hadn't even known existed. As if he saw deeper, further than anyone had before. It was equally exhilarating and frightening. "I think everyone has a part of themselves they keep private, but those aren't necessarily secrets."

Gage sat back and the spell, the intensity, the magic disappeared. "Interesting distinction. And what about you? Is there a husband or boyfriend back in the States who'll get his knickers in a twist because I'm standing in for Signora Ciavelli?"

She smiled at his phrasing and shook her head. Her heart skipped a beat because he was checking out her availability as surely as she'd checked out his. "No twisted knickers back in Atlanta."

"Now, that makes me wonder what's wrong with American men, rather than what's wrong with you," he said. His grin sent heat through her and awakened an aching desire deep inside her. However, she didn't miss the deft change of subject. "So the first order of business is shopping to replace your wardrobe?"

She'd been so caught up in their conversation, she'd nearly managed to forget about her clammy underwear. Now she was reminded of it in spades. She couldn't help squirming in her seat a little.

"The sooner the better. And I'm a quick shopper."

"I take it you're not interested in Gucci, Valentino or Versace?"

She'd grown up scraping pennies. A couple years of drought had set her father's farming operation in the red, and she'd learned to be thrifty by nature. And then, there was the whole high-fashion tie-in with her mother, which was all the more reason to eschew it. "Even if I had an interest, my budget wouldn't go there." She glanced down at her travel knits. They'd qualified as a splurge. "Are there any one-stop shopping stores?"

"There's Coin, a department store in the Cannaregio sestiere. Reasonably priced. They'd probably have the majority of what you want."

She recognized the name, thanks to the numerous guidebooks she'd read preparing herself for this trip. Cannaregio, the northern sestiere sandwiched between the upper *S* of the Grand Canal, Venice's central water route, and the outlying islands of Burano and Murano, contained the world's oldest ghetto. It had been home to Tintoretto, the prolific sixteenth-century artist, who was born, lived and died in Cannaregio and only left Venice once in his life. The history of this place amazed her.

"I believe I'm a Coin kind of shopper."

"Coin it is, then." He stood and pulled out her chair for her. She could get used to those little touches of gallantry. "Would you prefer to walk or take the vaporetto?"

She was all about walking, just as soon as she had on dry underwear. "Water bus, now. Walk, later."

He offered a smile and a half bow from the waist. "Your wish is my command," he said.

The comment sizzled through her.

She was beginning to think having Gage as a guide wasn't such a bad thing after all.

5

"I STILL CAN'T QUITE BELIEVE I'm actually here," the Gorgon, or Holly, as he needed to think of her since that's how she presented herself, said in that lilting Southern accent that transformed *here* to *he-ah*. She speared him with her wide aqua gaze as the large, crowded water bus moved north through the Grand Canal. The city's centuries-old crumbling splendor flanked them on both sides. The distinctive domes of St. Mark's Basilica rose behind them, but it was Holly who commanded his attention.

Her eyes shone and the wind ruffled her hair across her smooth cheek. For the odd second, Gage tried to recall a time when he'd felt so enthusiastic about anything.

Unfortunately none came to mind. He reminded himself it was simply an act on her part.

"Lovely, isn't it," he said, not necessarily talking about the scenery. For a woman who'd struck him as average when he'd first seen her, she appeared anything but with her shining eyes and wind-tossed hair.

Gage reminded himself the Gorgon had to be good to have been in the game this long. He'd noted her furtive examination of her cup and silverware at breakfast—a quick check for any residues indicating poisoning. He always did the same. However, he was fairly certain she hadn't pegged him as an agent. Her stab at him being a man with secrets was most probably a ruse she would've pulled with anyone, a test of sorts, an attempt to flush out another operative.

But there was a discordant note. All the pieces were there, but they didn't seem to mesh. She had quite obviously scanned every person walking into the pastry shop earlier, and now, despite her infatuation with the impressive palazzos lining the waterway, she continued to search the crowd.

There were two inherent pieces that didn't fit. Her watchfulness was too bloody…watchful. It lacked even a sophisticated, studied casualness. She seemed to search the sea of faces for one that was familiar. And then there was her sparkling, bright-eyed wonder with the city itself. That was damn near impossible to feign. She almost had him convinced she'd never traveled abroad before. However, according to the dossier he'd received upon briefing, the Gorgon had been sighted in both Prague and Helsinki since the first of the year.

And then there was a third piece that didn't fit. He was a master at reading people—facial expressions, body language, tonal inflections. He executed his observations logically, scientifically. With the Gorgon, it was as if that distance, that disconnect he felt with the rest of the world, had been ripped aside and he felt *her.* Not intellectually but emotionally, instinctively. And it was a reciprocal thing. It was as if she'd slipped beneath his skin, crawled inside him. As if, and here was a fanciful thought, he'd stumbled across the part of himself that had been missing since his parents' deaths. And wasn't that a bloody inconvenience, considering the Gorgon wouldn't hesitate to kill him if she thought he was a threat.

Gage lightly touched her elbow and leaned down a bit so she could hear him above the conversation flowing about them and the boat engine noise. Tendrils of her hair, set in motion by the breeze, danced against his face. He had the most insane urge to wrap his hands around her shoulders and bury his face in the silken mass. He was not, however, a man given to insane urges, and he ruthlessly quelled this one, contenting himself instead with lightly touching one shoulder and speaking in her ear. "We get off at the next stop."

A quarter hour later, they entered the department store, Coin, which could've been found in any European or American city. It brought to mind the London store Marks & Spencer. Holly stopped him at the door.

"You don't need to shop with me. I can meet you in an hour or so."

Hardly. Unfortunately, he couldn't follow her into the changing room, but other than that, she wouldn't be out of sight.

"There's nothing I'd rather do for the next hour than shop with you. You're my assignment this week." He offered what he hoped was a charming smile as he tossed her earlier assessment back at her. "It's the way we workaholics operate."

"I'm perfectly capable of picking out clothes by myself. Even I can navigate a department store." But despite whatever protestations she manufactured, he wasn't turning her loose in the store.

"I can offer the unique male perspective. How can you forfeit that opportunity?"

Clever humor sparkled in her eyes. "I doubt there's much that's unique about *any* male perspective—forget comfort and go for the briefest thing available."

His bark of laughter was spontaneous. "Touché. So, it's possibly not terribly unique, after all."

Mirth shaded her eyes, making them more blue than green. "Maybe I'm not concerned with the male perspective."

"Then consider this an opportunity to educate me on what women like. I can benefit from observing female choice as made with absolute disregard for the male perspective."

"You don't give up, do you?"

"I've been told it's part of my charm."

"Someone lied to you." She laughed, relenting. "Okay. Whatever. You want to shop with me, far be it from me to deprive you of the experience. Let's go."

The first section they came to happened to be undergarments. A thong display stood front and center. It was rather difficult to ignore the array of abbreviated knickers in various colors and patterns.

Holly slanted him an arch look. "The merchandising was obviously arranged by a man. Let me guess—these rank as a first pick from your unique male perspective."

"Actually, being a male—" and possessing both the equipment and the imagination "—I must say I appreciate the art form…." Holly groaned at him and looked as if she'd like to toss something at his head. "I can't say it appears very comfortable." Walking around with a string bisecting one's bum all day looked like some sort of self-inflicted torture.

The Gorgon's retort was lost as a store attendant walked up to them.

"Buon giorno," she greeted them. "May I help you?" she asked in English, no doubt having heard them conversing.

While Holly nattered on to the woman about lost luggage and her requirements, Gage mentally registered all the shoppers in their vicinity. They hadn't picked up a tail en route, he was sure of that. And the only slightly suspicious person was a woman, dark hair covered by a scarf, mid-twenties, sunglasses, pushing a pram one section over. Weren't babies generally noisy and messy? As if on cue, the little bugger wailed. The woman was legitimate.

The attendant bypassed the thong display. Pursing her mouth, her head held to one side, she assessed Holly. Then she selected a pair of low-cut black knickers trimmed in lace. It would be a good look on Holly's well-rounded hips and bottom. His cock stirred at the idea.

"You like?" The attendant directed the question to him, rather than Holly. Obviously she'd pegged them as a couple, and in light of Holly's earlier assertion that she could pick out her own clothes, it struck him as humorous that she was now being excluded from the equation.

"Very much. Sexy yet practical." That rather summed up Holly herself. He quirked an inquiring eyebrow at her. "And the independent female verdict is?"

She shot him a look he couldn't quite interpret and deliberately addressed the attendant. "I'll take seven pairs."

"Buono. And the—" She gestured toward Holly's breasts.

Gage bit back a grin and glanced away, affording her a moment of privacy. He might be doing a fine job of mentally outfitting her in the knickers and a bra, but he wasn't going to ogle her in a public place.

The woman brought over a matching bra in a sheer black material trimmed in lace and held it up for their approval. "Nice, no?"

It certainly appealed to him, some parts of him more than others. "It speaks to this not-so-unique male."

The Gorgon all but laughed. "And it's saying?"

"A resounding yes."

"I'm shocked."

There was something to be said for a woman with a dry wit.

The attendant glanced from Holly, to him, and back to Holly, clearly at a loss with the byplay. Holly nodded. "Si, one please."

"Nightgown, *si?*" the attendant inquired, and Holly nodded again.

"Yes, I need a nightgown."

Rows of nightgowns, robes and jammies were adjacent to the undergarments, offering an extensive assortment of style and color—long, short, demure and provocative.

Gage waited to see what she'd select. He'd immediately spotted his choice.

Instead, Holly chose a plain cream nightshirt. Definitely not what a woman with her lovely back should wear. And if he had to monitor her, definitely not what he wanted to see her in while he watched.

"But this matches your eyes." He plucked the silk nightgown shot through in shades of greens and blues that boasted narrow straps along with a plunging neckline and an open back. His look dared her.

"*Si, si. Perfecto.*" The woman snatched the cream nightshirt from Holly and returned it to the rack, shaking her head and making a tsking sound, a frown knitting her eyebrows. "Not for you."

The attendant took the garment from Gage and held it

in front of Holly, turning her to view herself in the mirror. It was easy enough to imagine her with her clothes off and the gown on. In fact, it was bloody impossible not to. The generous swell of her breasts, the indentation of her trim waist, the sensuous curve of her hips…

Her gaze snared his in the mirror. Hadn't his orders been to seduce her if necessary? Desire arced between them. It was simply a matter of time….

"I'll take it." Her husky Southern voice stroked over him, through him. "And the matching robe."

Orders or not, it'd be damned embarrassing to walk about with a hard-on. And impossible to hide. He thrust the image of Holly in the nightie firmly from his mind.

Despite those seemingly guileless eyes, the biggest mistake he could make would be to underestimate Holly. The Gorgon was one dangerous woman.

"WHERE WOULD YOU LIKE IT?" Gage asked as he closed her hotel room door behind them.

Holly caught her lower lip between her teeth. Just because she'd developed a crush on Gage Carswell didn't mean she had to read sex into everything. But it was very, very difficult not to do just that when every look, every brush of his arm, not to mention his scent, all led her down that path of sensual wanting.

And it intensified things. Even though she disliked shopping, she'd found it…stimulating to shop with him.

When she'd checked in last night, her room had seemed rather narrow. Now it shrank to intimate proportions. Daylight sifted through the slats of the shuttered window. The lyrical notes of Italian conversation, punctuated by the occasional shout, drifted up from outside, accentuating their seclusion. She snapped on the bedside lamp to dispel the shadowed intimacy.

Gage stood, waiting, his obsidian eyes unrevealing. Oh, yeah. Where'd she want her suitcase? "On the bed would be great."

She'd meant to sound all crisp and businesslike. She'd aimed for the same tone she used at the beginning of school when she established rules for her students. Instead her words had come out all soft and breathy.

"The bed it is," he said.

They'd packed her purchases into her new suitcase, which, given Venice's uneven stone streets and stairs, had been hell to haul despite the luggage wheels. Well, it had been hell to haul until Gage had insisted on carrying it. Holly was an independent woman, but she wasn't a stupid one. She'd relinquished it. She'd be sure to put a little extra toward Gage's tip when the trip was over.

And the man had handled it as if it were nothing. He hadn't even broken a sweat. Not that she wanted to stereotype anyone, but she hadn't expected a guy who owned an art gallery to be so fit. She suspected there must be muscle hidden beneath his shirt. She had an almost burning need to find out. In a very short time, Gage Carswell had lit a very hot flame inside her.

He started to move past her, and in trying to get out of his way, she moved in the wrong direction and bumped into him.

"Here. Let me make this easier." Holly backed up to the wall, the plaster rough and uneven against her fingertips as she pressed against it.

Good grief, he smelled good. Not that overwhelming, clog-your-sinuses douse of men's cologne, but a faint blend of soap and man. She had a keen sense of smell, and some aromas didn't sit well with her. But she liked his scent. *Like* was the wrong word—it was too insipid. His scent triggered a primal feminine chord in her. It was as if his yang called forth her yin. This feeling, this arousal of the senses, was obviously what advertisers tried so desperately to capture in all those ads.

Gage lifted her suitcase to the edge of the bed. "Are you an unpacker or do you prefer to keep your things in your case?"

"I'll unpack, since I'm going to be here several days."

"Shall I lend a hand? It'll go faster."

Maybe she was sick and depraved but she liked the idea of having him touch her underwear. What she'd like better was the idea of him touching *her*, but she hadn't quite worked that out yet, so she'd settle with him handling her panties. Besides she hadn't missed the look in his eyes when they'd been shopping. It upped the ante.

"Sure. You can hand off to me." She opened the chifforobe, which stood slightly off-center to the bottom of the bed and pulled out one of the two drawers inside the cabinet. "Ready."

She'd spent her entire morning with Gage and was well aware that the top of her head came nearly even with his shoulder. But standing so close in her tiny hotel room gave her a new appreciation for the width of his shoulders. He handed off the pants and tops she'd bought to wear during the day.

"You're pleased with your purchases?" he asked, his fingers brushing hers as he passed them to her.

She smiled to hide the tremor that accompanied his fleeting touch. If he touched more than her hand with something other than a casual brush of his fingers…the mere idea threatened her composure.

"I'd prefer to have not spent the money, but yes, I'm very pleased. These clothes are a better cut than what I had." She put the garments away and closed the drawer.

After pulling out the other drawer, she turned to him again. He held the nightgown and robe, but didn't relinquish it. It was as if he wanted to admire it a little longer. "This will be stunning with your eyes." And though he didn't say it, she could clearly read it in *his* eyes that he thought it would be stunning with the rest of her, as well.

"It was a good spot on your part. It must be your artistic eye."

"I told you I'd be helpful." His smile set her pulse thundering. "And from the male perspective, that's definitely a winner."

"Ah, the all-important male viewpoint," she teased.

He passed along the underwear. "And these, as well. Just to reiterate."

"I would've thought, strictly from the male perspective, the thong would've been the winner."

He grinned and made a tsking sound. "Ah, the weight of representing the male population. Sometimes more is better. Despite what popular culture might lead one to believe, there's much to be said for a hint of what hides beneath rather than a shout-out."

He pulled out a dress, a jersey in shades of blues and greens and a pair of strappy black sandals that weren't nearly as practical as what she'd originally packed. But then, she hadn't known Gage Carswell would be dropped into her world the first time she'd packed. And Gage brought out a part of her that was far more sensual than practical.

"This is a beautiful illustration of sensual and seductive," he said, picking up the nightgown again and finally passing it to her.

"But you haven't seen it on." She hadn't set foot outside of the dressing room.

"I have a very active…imagination."

Well, hers was pretty activated right about now. She didn't have a bit of trouble imagining the way his mouth would feel against hers. "I'm sure that comes in handy."

Could she have come back with some sophisticated, witty repartee? Apparently not. She had to throw out something scintillating like *handy*.

"Handy? It does, as a matter of fact, now and then."

He had her in such a state she couldn't even think straight. She'd better send him to his room before she made a total fool of herself. "I've got it from here," she said, tucking the gown into the drawer with her undergarments.

"You're sure? I don't mind lending a hand."

"Thanks. I can manage to undress myself."

"I meant the toiletries in your case."

Way to go, Holly. Too late on the "making a total fool" aspect. She'd just hit that homerun. "Right. I knew that. I can manage everything on my own." She smiled brightly while she practically shoved him through the bathroom door. And though embarrassed, she still couldn't help noticing his back and arms were rock-solid beneath her hands.

His unfailingly polite smile didn't disguise the hint of wickedness just below the surface. "Just give a rap on the door when you're ready."

"Will do." She kept her smile firmly in place until he closed the door behind him.

Well. Open mouth and insert foot. *I can manage to undress myself.* Talk about a manifestation of subconscious desire.

She quickly stripped off the clothes she'd been wearing and the still-damp underwear. The air in the room chilled her naked skin, but it was a vast improvement over wearing dirty clothes. She opened the drawer for a pair of clean panties and her hand brushed the silk of her new gown.

She hadn't tried it on at the store. Giving in to impulse, she slipped it on over her head. The silk whispered against her skin as it settled over her in a sensual glide. She looked in the mirror mounted above the desk.

It could've been custom-made for her, the way it show-cased her breasts and flowed over her hips with the split up the left side to mid-thigh. No frilly lace or bows, it boasted clean, elegant lines while being very sexy. She turned to the right and then to the left, admiring the way she looked in it. She loved it.

Her heart thudded heavily. Gage had picked this out for her. For the first time, she realized how arousing it was having a man decide that you belonged in something so alluring. Desire radiated from her core in a slow, insistent throb. She shrugged into the robe and loosely tied the sash at her waist.

What would Gage think if he saw her now? What would he do?

She knew exactly what she wanted him to do…. Closing her eyes, she imagined the scenario she was suddenly so desperate to experience.

She crossed the room and opened the shutters. Sunlight and fresh air shifted against her skin.

She sensed him the moment he stepped into the room, the way an animal in the wild senses a mate. She tensed but didn't turn around. He padded over to stand behind her, his scent and warmth enveloping her even before he touched her. Her body quivered with anticipation, each nerve ending primed for his touch. He wrapped his arms around her from behind. The air was cool, his touch warm.

Her heart hammered against her ribs as he slowly, deliberately untied the knot holding her robe together. It gave way and the garment fell open. Without a word, he reached up and slid the silky material over her shoulders and down her arms, leaving it to fall and puddle between their feet in a sensual heap. Her nipples peaked and hardened at the onslaught of the breeze and the warmth of his body behind hers. They stood in the window, where anyone who happened to glance up might see them.

His every move marked by sensual deliberation, he stroked his hands up and over her silk-covered belly until he cupped her breasts. With a whispered sigh, he drew her back against his hard, muscular length. The ridge of his erection nestled against her buttocks as he grazed his thumbs over her nipples in a gossamer-light touch.

Words weren't necessary. Even though the cadence and rhythm of his voice aroused her, words had become extemporaneous. The sights and sounds of Venice surrounded them in drifts of conversation and an Italian aria in the distance, a sensual drama that gave voice to what was unfolding between them.

She placed her hands over his, the masculine smattering of hair rough against her palms. Her breath quickened. He bent his head to that sensitive juncture where her neck and shoulder met. His breath warmed her skin, the faint scrub of his beard arousing as he nuzzled the spot that made her feel as if all of her bones were melting beneath the touch of his mouth.

He brought his right hand up over her collarbone and along the line of her neck. Cupping her jaw, he turned her head and scattered hot kisses along her shoulder up her neck, until his mouth angled over hers. His lips sampled hers like a butterfly sampling a flower's nectar. As if her bud pleased him, he kissed her again, this time his lips clinging, lingering, drinking. Her mouth blossomed beneath his and his tongue probed its recesses even as he skimmed his hand against the needy tip of her breast.

When she thought it was safe to relax and give herself over to the sensation coursing through her, she tasted it against her tongue in his mouth, felt it in his touch, sensed it with a part of her being that seemed connected to him on another plane, another level. The edge of danger. The darkness. And while it frightened her, it turned her on even more. It heightened her senses to a new level. Making love with him would be unlike anything she'd ever experienced. Her body ached with an unfilled need, a desire to have him lean her over his arm, bow her back, to feel the rasp of his beard against her breasts as he tugged her aching nipple into his mouth…

A sharp rap on the door shattered the moment. "Holly? Everything okay?" Concern roughened his voice.

"I'm…" She paused and swallowed the husky note of desire. "I'm fine. Just changing. Give me a minute."

"Right. Just checking."

She wasn't sure whether to thank him or kill him.

6

GAGE PLOWED HIS HAND through his hair. Christ, the woman was killing him. Finally, she was out of that damned nightgown and into her new trousers and top. He couldn't stop himself from rapping on her door. How much could a man take? And he'd been incapable of looking away...even though he knew she wasn't making a phone call, knew she wasn't leaving a message or looking for information. Still, it could only be to his benefit if Holly, the Gorgon, was sexually frustrated. Frustration often led to carelessness. A little frustration might lend him the break he needed. Aroused but unsatisfied was precisely where he wanted her. Unfortunately, it was precisely where he found himself, as well.

Had she been instructed to seduce him or anyone else who might help her while in Venice? Did it really matter? Confident she'd left no message nor retrieved any package, he turned off his monitor. Almost immediately, she knocked on his door and waited.

Odd, that. He would've expected the Gorgon to offer the perfunctory knock and then enter. One never knew what could be discovered with an element of surprise.

He opened the washroom door. "Ready?"

The monitor afforded a clear picture of her, but it didn't

adequately reflect her hair's gloss or her eyes' luminosity. It certainly didn't relay her scent or that slight hitch in her breath when she faced him. In a perfect world, that would all leave him patently unaffected. Unfortunately, the world remained imperfect. He felt her impact from his head to his toes.

She moistened her lips with the tip of her tongue. "We need to discuss a few things before we go. Your room or mine?"

He supposed it'd be asking too much that she might waltz in and reveal all her spy secrets and they'd simply be done. *That* he'd be excited about. But in his experience, when a woman wanted to talk, what followed was generally dreadful.

"Certainly. I'd love a chat." Right up there with picking up a burr in his backside. "My room is fine." This could be a ploy to check out his quarters. Or perhaps she intended planting an audio bug in his room. He'd watch her like a hawk.

He stood aside and ushered her in. "Have a seat." He pulled the chair out for her. He'd much rather position himself on the bed than have her sit there. Well, actually, he wouldn't mind positioning himself *on* her, he just meant it was better he sit on the bed than have to see her sitting on his bed. Christ, she'd muddled his thinking.

She perched on the edge of the chair, bracing her hands on the edge. He'd be damn sure to check beneath that chair for any plants.

He settled on the corner of the bed, his knee nearly touching hers.

"I suppose you've had an opportunity to look at the itinerary I submitted," she said.

"Yes." She'd picked up a fragrance at the cosmetic counter. It was subtle. He wasn't so good at discerning perfume components, but this scent made him think of open-mouthed kisses, tangled limbs and sex-tumbled sheets. But back to the itinerary… "You have some interesting choices. Most people want to immediately tour St. Mark's, the Doge's Palace, the Rialto with all of its shops." Aside from the canals, the places he'd mentioned were the primary tourist draws, but they didn't factor into Holly's itinerary until later in the week.

"I know. That's what we need to discuss." She drew a deep breath and glanced down, her lashes, no longer gold-tipped due to a coating of newly purchased mascara, formed crescents against her cheeks. She looked back up. "I'm kind of here to look for someone."

Bloody hell. Perhaps he should ring Agnes to purchase a lotto ticket for him. It looked as if today might be his lucky day, after all.

"I see." He leaned forward, bracing his arms on his knees and loosely linking his fingers. It was a casual pose designed to invite sharing confidences. "And are they expecting you?"

She shook her head and worried her lower lip between her teeth. "Not exactly."

He wished she wouldn't abuse her lovely lip that way. It made him want to capture her mouth with his and suck on the teeth marks she'd left behind, lick at it…. If she was trying to distract him, she was bang-on.

"Not exactly?" he repeated.

"Well, not at all."

"I see." He didn't have a sodding clue what she was talking about. Yet. But he didn't want to say too much and spook her. Her back and shoulders were rigid, her expression guarded, but she exhibited none of the subtle-yet-telltale signs of lying he was trained to identify. "And do you know where to find this person?"

She shifted in her seat. "I have an idea."

"The idea being the itinerary?"

"Pretty much." She pushed her hair behind one ear and he noted she had small, well-shaped ears with only a hint of a lobe, single holes pierced in each. "I'm sorry. I don't mean to be cryptic. This just feels so awkward. I thought I'd have Signora Ciavelli, and as a woman, she'd understand." Her inhalation was sharp in the room's quiet.

This was going to be good. He was breathless to see just how inventive a lie she manufactured. After all, Holly was the Gorgon. She wasn't about to drop the truth in his lap.

She reached in her knapsack and he tensed, prepared to disarm her if she pulled out a weapon.

But she didn't. She produced a photo, frayed and yellowed around the edges, and offered it to him. He held it in the flat of his palm. No need to offer up unnecessary fingerprints.

She set aside the knapsack.

He examined the photo of a brunette. Tall, slender. Classic bone structure. Cool smile. Judging by her clothes and the car bonnet behind her, he'd estimate the snapshot to be twenty-five to thirty years old. He looked up from the woman in the photo to the woman in the chair. "You're looking for her?"

"She's my mother."

Righto. He didn't know who the woman was but he'd wager it wasn't *her* mum. The woman in the photo was strikingly beautiful. The woman in the chair, aside from her eyes, was strikingly average. One bore no resemblance to the other.

"It sounds as if there's a story to tell." Go ahead, Madam Gorgon, and weave your tangled web. He passed the photo back to her.

"My mother was a fashion model working with some of the top houses when she met my father. It was a whirlwind romance—they met, they married. He carted her back to his farm in Georgia and before long, she was pregnant with my brother. It was like *Green Acres* without the comedic scriptwriters." She offered a mocking smile. He had no idea what *Green Acres* was, but he nodded nonetheless so she'd continue. "Oddly enough, all was not well in paradise and they made the decision that's always so confounded me. They decided having another kid was just the way to fix their broken marriage. People do crazy things." She shook her head and snapped back from where she'd seemed to lose herself in introspection. "Long story short. I came along. I was three when my mother was offered work at a photo shoot in Venice. She said she'd be gone a week. That was twenty-seven years ago."

She was convincingly good. Her delivery held just enough dispassion and detachment to infer a lifetime of hurt and rejection. A sparkle of tears shone in her eyes but were held in check. The defiant tilt of her head dared him to ask her if she cared. If he didn't know it all to be a lie, he might well ache for the small girl abandoned by her mother.

He played it as if he bought her story. "I'm sorry, Holly." He reached out and brushed his fingers against her face, much as he might stroke a frightened kitten. She leaned slightly into his touch, her cheek as soft as down against his fingertips. His heart thudded heavily in his chest and he reminded himself it was all an act. He dropped his hand to his side. "You've kept in touch? You know she's here?"

She shook her head. "Apparently, my father kept up with her whereabouts and what she was doing, although he never mentioned it to us kids. I guess he thought it would just upset us. Personally, I think he kept hoping she'd finally come home to us. It only took twenty-five years for him to figure out that wasn't going to happen and that he needed to move on with his life. He stopped tracking her last year. At that time she lived in the Dorsoduro area."

"Do you remember anything about her?"

She pulled her feet up on the chair rung, drawing her knees up. She suddenly looked like the awkward, abandoned child in her tale. "Do I remember her tucking me into bed? Kissing a skinned knee? Teaching me to tie my shoes? No. As funny as it seems, I remember the way she smelled. For years, I would feel all tight inside if I caught a whiff of this certain perfume. Last year, when my father was getting remarried, I helped him clean out the cabinet under the bathroom sink. There was an old, dusty perfume bottle she'd left behind. One whiff and that's when I put it all together. It was her scent."

She smiled self-consciously, as if she'd said too much, revealed too much, and planted her feet back on the floor. "I've got a good sniffer. I recognized your scent this morning even before you said this was your room." She tucked the photograph back into her bag. "I know I don't look anything like her. I take after my father's side of the family, but my brother is her spitting image."

Wasn't that a convenient excuse for a total absence of family resemblance? He wondered if she'd come up with that sad tale all on her own or if their organization had picked up a scriptwriter.

However, he couldn't quite dismiss a nagging sense of truth behind her story. He'd glimpsed raw, naked pain in her eyes, recognizing it as something he'd felt long, long ago. He *knew* what that look felt like. He'd spent years forgetting what that felt like.

"Actually, no, you don't look like her. She doesn't have your fantastic eyes and it doesn't sound as if she has your substance, either." She might be the enemy, but she had to possess a great deal of strength to have lasted in this business as long as she had.

She regarded him with guileless eyes. It was like looking into the depths of an ocean of surprise…and vulnerability. "That's a nice thing to say."

He knew who she was and what she was. So why, then, did he have the totally inane feeling he needed to protect her from him? He swatted away the notion as if it were a pesky fly. Finding and exploiting the Gorgon's weaknesses was his job.

"It's not nice. It's simply the truth. They're not always the same, you know."

"No, they're not, are they." She lowered her eyelids and leaned forward, a classic invitation to a kiss. Were she any other woman, he'd almost peg it as a subconscious move.

He curved his fingers around the velvet skin at the nape of her neck, her hair shifting against his knuckles like a fall of silk. Her lips parted.

She slid her fingers into his hair, molding them against

his scalp. "Could this get you into trouble?" she murmured in that soft dulcet voice even as she tugged him closer.

"Hmm. Strictly against company policy."

"I don't want you to compromise—"

He quieted her with a finger to her lips' pillowy softness. "Some things are worth the risk," he murmured as he angled his head and kissed her.

It was best to stick as close to the truth as possible.

HIS MOUTH GRAZED HERS and then settled. He was a good kisser. He had a nice technique, not too wet, not too dry, not sloppy or any of the other things that could ruin a potentially good kiss but the bottom line was that he just wasn't into it, which meant she wasn't particularly into it if she could sit here and put together a mental evaluation. Yeah, that was problematic…and disappointing. She'd felt such an instant attraction—

Whoa! While she'd been evaluating mid-kiss, he obviously found his groove, because in an instant, he shifted from ho-hum to magic!

Coherent thought deserted her and Holly gave herself up to the sensation of his mouth on hers, the warm press of his fingers against her skin, the slow tumble into a lethargy that threatened to buckle her knees.

Gage broke the kiss. "We need to leave. Now."

Holly reluctantly opened her eyes and let the magic sift away. Another kiss like that would lead to another and another. It would be just a matter of time until they were on the bed and kisses would lead to touching and touching would lead to clothes coming off and clothes coming off would lead to… Holly knew she had a tendency to jump too quickly into relationships, but even this was fast for her. "Yes. We should leave."

One simple kiss—well it was more along the lines of one very complicated kiss—and she felt punch-drunk. Kissing Gage Carswell was heady stuff.

"So, you're pleased with your new purchases?" he asked as he locked the door behind them.

Holly was only momentarily taken aback by his abrupt subject switch, as if they hadn't just had a close call. She'd been raised by males. She knew that most men didn't want to "talk something to death," and sometimes, a mere mention fell into the "talk to death" category.

"They're clean and dry—a vast improvement over what I had on. So yes, I'm pleased."

"That outfit looks very nice on you."

They walked down the hall, wall sconces lending filtered light. The Pensione Armand abutted two buildings on either side and all the windows were in the guest rooms, leaving the hallway dimly lit. It was one of those moments that she knew she'd remember forever. The pools of light, the worn rose-patterned carpet underfoot, the faint aroma of lemon wax combined with the scent particular to Gage, the taste of him that lingered on her mouth, his hand at her elbow.

They descended the stairs in silence. Watercolors and oils of Venice were interspersed along the stair wall, some obviously older than others, some far more skillfully executed. Finally Gage broke the silence. "Are you anxious about making contact…with your mum?"

Holly had the oddest sensation there was something she was missing. She shrugged it off as they descended the last of the stairs into the empty lobby area. "Maybe."

"Are you sure you know where to begin looking?"

"My father had a pretty good way of knowing where she could be found."

Gage quirked a dark, heavy eyebrow in question. "A private detective." She laughed, more in amazement than in humor. She still found it difficult to believe. "My father, this practical down-to-earth guy who'd always been so careful with his money—" God, she could remember bad-crop years when there hadn't been a cent to buy new clothes for school. While all the other girls had shown up with at least a couple of new outfits, she'd made do with what she'd worn the previous year or what they could find at the thrift shop. "This is the man who kept up with Julia through a private detective. How pathetic is that? Years and years afterward, he kept thinking one day she'd miss us enough to come back. And he never mentioned her to us. As if we'd forgotten we had a mother who'd walked out." Holly was really angry. She didn't know why and she wasn't even sure who that anger was directed toward, but she felt nauseous all the same. It was her worst failing that when she got really upset or scared, she threw up. And she'd look totally pathetic if she puked now.

For years she'd endured the pitying looks from others. But she'd rather amputate a limb than look pathetic. She'd own neurotic but pathetic…never!

Gage held the lobby door open and she stepped out into the bright sun and exotic air that held the scents of Venice—the tinge of saltwater, the scent of fresh baked bread, a slight dankness that came from being surrounded by water, and something undescribable that had to be the product of hundreds of years of footprints and people living and dying in a place.

And what had happened to her that she'd blurted out all the intimate details of her life to a man she'd just met? Why'd she feel this link to someone who was virtually a stranger?

What was wrong with her? Everything seemed to be out of sync, her reaction to Gage, to the city, that kiss…. "What about you? Do you have one parent that secretly stalks another? What skeletons lurk in your closet?"

They set out to the left. "No stalking. No skeletons. Both of my parents were killed when I was a lad. I ended up at boarding school."

That yanked her out of her own problems. "Oh, God. How awful." She could almost feel the gaping hole inside him. "Did you have any other family?"

He shrugged. "I was luckier than some. I didn't find myself on the street or in an orphanage. I had my grandfather. He arranged for my schooling."

Where she came from, boarding schools were decidedly elitist. Certainly nobody she knew had ever gone. Did it mean the same thing in the U.K.? "Did you live at school or with your grandfather?"

"School. I spent holidays with the Colonel, generally rather miserable affairs. He never quite reconciled with the idea that I'd survived what my parents hadn't."

At least she'd had her father, her brother, Kyle, her grandmother and cousin, Josephine, after a fashion. She read so much into Gage's story that it was painful. She wanted to reach over and touch her hand to his, but his facial expression didn't invite gestures of comfort.

"That couldn't have been fun."

"It was a long time ago and it was what it was," he said in a dismissive tone, letting it go with a shrug and a hollow smile.

Curiosity gnawed at her, but his closed expression didn't invite further questions.

The more she knew about him, the more she wanted to know. She was certain there was much more to Gage Carswell than met the eye.

7

THEY STOOD ON THE OTHER side of the picturesque canal outside the house and Holly's heart raced. It was imposing, her mother's home. Certainly not as grand as the palazzos they'd passed in the Grand Canal, but grand enough.

She pulled her camera out of her backpack and glanced at Gage, who stood silently next to her. "You're sure that's it?"

"Positive."

"I'm taking a picture to show Kyle."

"Kyle?"

"My brother."

"Ah. I see."

She stepped back and zoomed out, aiming to get as much of the background in as possible—the canal lined with small boats moored to the large poles thrusting out of the water, the stone landing and the short broad stairs that led up to the stone street. The three-story house washed in a faded pink was rich in an architectural style that Holly didn't recognize. One large balcony fashioned of intricate wrought iron dominated the center of the second floor, flanked by two smaller auxiliary ones. The third floor, while lacking the accompanying smaller balconies, also boasted a large one in its center, yet the wrought-iron pattern was more open and fluid. The roof bore the red tiles she'd noticed on many other buildings and a distinct rounded chimney.

She snapped the photo and then zoomed in for a few close-ups. This structure was a far cry from the white clapboard farmhouse she and Kyle had grown up in, the one her father still lived in.

"Shall I snap a photo of you?"

"Oh, no." She hated having her picture taken. Just about the time she thought she looked pretty good, she'd see a photo and realize she still needed to drop ten, well, make it fifteen, pounds. She almost suggested taking his photo instead. It would be the most natural thing in the world to take a picture of her guide as a reminder of her time in Venice, except it felt too soon and too intimate to ask him. That's because she knew in her heart that when she looked at his photograph, she wouldn't be seeing him as just a guide.

She shoved her camera into her backpack.

"What now? Shall we stroll over to the Ca'Rezzonico?"

They'd lunched at an open-air café in the sprawling Campo Santa Margherita. She'd loved the mix of homes dating back to the fourteenth and fifteenth centuries, the small, offbeat shops and all the market stalls selling everything from live eels and lobsters to a colorful array of fresh vegetables. But she'd also constantly scanned the crowds for a woman who might be Julia. If they went to the Ca'Rezzonico, the furnished Baroque palace open to public tours, she wouldn't be able to concentrate and do it proper justice.

She shook her head. "I want to go to my mother's house. I need to get Julia out of the way."

"Do you want to call first on your mobile?"

"No." It came out sharp and abrupt. "Sorry, I didn't mean to snap. I've just seen, firsthand, that calling ahead can backfire."

"You don't want her to have the opportunity to tell you not to show up?"

"Exactly." She smiled, trying to relieve some of the tension curled inside her like a tight spring. "If I'd wanted to call, I could've stayed home." But she didn't. She wanted to see this woman face-to-face. "I want to walk over there and knock on her door."

"Very well, then. Let's go knock."

They walked without further conversation down the street and crossed the small stone footbridge spanning the canal. They made their way back up to the house with the double front doors and the gargoyle door knocker. She was nervous.

"Are you okay?"

No. No, she wasn't okay at all. Sweat coated her palms and nausea gripped her. "I'm fine. Just taking a moment." God knows, she'd run through this countless times in her head and now she was drawing a blank.

She breathed deeply. Above, the sky glittered a brilliant sunlit cerulean blue and pigeons cooed. Holly took it as an omen.

"If you'd like to do something else for a while, I can meet you afterward." She felt as if she should exonerate him from having to see this…heck, she didn't even know what to call it. Was it a reunion? A confrontation? An exorcism?

"You haven't met her yet. You don't know what her family is like or how many of them there might be. You've no idea how they'll receive you. I think I should accompany you."

A measure of relief sifted through her, a sense of calm replacing some of the anxiety that had her heart racing. Granted, she still didn't know, now that the time was almost upon her, exactly what she wanted to say. Maybe it was the common bond of speaking English in Italy, maybe it was the fact that she'd spent all of her waking time with him, and she didn't discount the kiss they'd shared, but she felt, perhaps ridiculously, as if she had a friend by her side rather than simply a paid companion. That idea did much to lend her self-confidence and calm.

"I'd like that."

"Then, as you Yanks say, let's do this thing."

Holly laughed, releasing yet more tension. Gage Carswell was good to have around.

She knocked on the door, and within a minute, it opened to reveal a woman who was obviously not Julia. Julia could've gained the forty pounds this woman carried, but she couldn't have lost the twelve inches in height.

All this time Holly had waited and now she found herself speechless. Beside her, Gage spoke in Italian. The woman cast a glance at the two of them, spoke briefly to Gage and closed the door in their face.

"I told her we had business to discuss with the lady of the house. She's gone to check if the mistress is available. Her words not mine."

"Thank you. I just froze."

Gage had a funny, almost perplexed look on his face. "It happens to the best of us sometimes."

"I have a hard time believing you'd ever freeze." She was nearly sick with apprehension. Their pointless chitchat was a welcome distraction. "You seem very adept at handling any situation."

His grin held an edge. "I'm sure my day will come."

Before Holly could reply, the door opened again and the woman invited them in. Holly stepped inside and the blood pounded in her head so hard she barely noticed the decor of the house.

They followed the woman down a rather dark hallway to a room near the back, and Holly's clammy hands began to shake. The woman ushered them into a high-ceilinged room, heavy with ornate carvings and velvet corded drapes.

An older, more mature version of the snapshot Holly carried in her purse rose gracefully from a sofa. Julia. Even if she hadn't looked the same, Holly would've recognized her scent. Her stomach constricted in response. Julia glanced at them both but addressed Gage.

"Paola says you have business you wish to discuss with me?" She spoke English in a throaty contralto.

Calm descended over Holly. Even though Julia had spoken to Gage, Holly answered. "I'm your daughter, Holly Noelle."

Other than a brief start of surprise, Julia's expression didn't change. She canted her head to one side and regarded Holly, arching one perfect eyebrow. "You look like your father."

"I'm aware of that."

"I've been expecting you," Julia said, her tone cool. There was no mistaking her arrival as a welcomed event.

"You have? Did Daddy—my father—contact you?"

Julia looked down her nose. "Good heavens, no. I haven't spoken to Charles in nearly thirty years."

How about twenty-seven years, two months and thirteen days? But Holly kept those figures to herself. There was something in Holly's knowing the exact figures that gave Julia even more power. "Then how could you possibly know I was coming?"

She shrugged, an elegant albeit indifferent gesture. "I felt sure curiosity would lead you here eventually." Her eyes assessed Gage. "Is this your brother?"

Not *my son,* but *your brother.* Holly didn't miss the distinction. And how could she even think Gage might be her son? Didn't she know that Kyle looked just like her?

"No. This is—"

Gage startled her by slipping an arm around her shoulders and interrupting, "One very lucky bloke. I'm her fiancé, Gage Carswell. Just proposed yesterday and she said yes."

"Ah, British." Julia narrowed her eyes slightly. "I knew you didn't look as if you came off the farm. Please, have a seat." Julia waved a hand in a grudging invitation.

She sank back onto the sofa upholstered in tangerine velvet. Holly and Gage shared a matching love seat.

"Shall I have Paola bring in some coffee? Tea?"

"No. Nothing for me." Tea or coffee on top of the nausea she was experiencing would finish her off.

"Nor me."

"Well, then, what can I do for you?" She crossed one long leg over the other.

Holly fought to hold on to her calm. *What could she do for her?* For starters she could drop to her damn-elegant knees and beg forgiveness for walking out on them. Or how about saying that after one glimpse of her daughter's face, she realized she'd made a horrible mistake? She could do that, but it seemed highly unlikely her mother would cooperate. Holly would have to settle for answers.

"Why did you leave and never come back?"

Julia looked at her as if Holly was simpleminded. "I left because I had a second chance at a career that I loved and thought I'd lost forever. I never came back because I was unhappy on that dreadful farm. Marrying Charles was a mistake. Why compound it by returning?"

"Maybe because you had two children?"

That question merited another look that said Julia had clearly birthed a dimwit. "But I was unhappy. I wouldn't have made a very good mother if I were unhappy. Living in the country was like being buried alive. Charles was never going to leave, so there really was no other option."

Gage's arm tightened around Holly's shoulders in silent support. "So, you just left? Just like that?"

"It seemed cleaner and neater for everyone involved. Charles couldn't afford to ferry you and your brother back and forth to Europe and neither could I. As well, my job didn't accommodate small children."

Holly felt as if one of her father's cows had kicked her in the gut. It was really no more complicated than that. They'd been discarded like unstylish outfits. "He has a name. My brother, *your son,* has a name. Kyle." She reached for her purse to pull out the pictures Sherrie had sent along, determined Julia would look at her son, at the man he'd become and the family he held dear.

A young woman, Holly would put her in her mid-twenties, breezed into the room on a cloud of perfume and energy. She was a dark-eyed beauty, stylishly dressed, her fall of long hair as dark and glossy as a raven's wing. "Mama—"

She stopped short, obviously surprised to see visitors.

"Bella, this is Holly and Gage. They're visiting Venice and dropped by. I knew Holly's father several years ago. This is my step-daughter, Bella."

They exchanged cursory greetings, then Bella said something to Julia in Italian and left. Despite the preceding conversation and the last twenty-seven years, Holly reeled at having been introduced as a nonentity. Although why that should upset her at this juncture… Quiet fury rippled through her and she left the photos in her purse.

"When I married Salvatore, my husband, he came with Bella and Bella came with a nanny." She offered a nonchalant shrug.

Holly stood abruptly. She was done here. "Thank you for your time."

Gage stood and wrapped his arm around her waist. Holly could've kissed him for the support in that one simple gesture.

Julia seemed impervious to her sarcasm and responded with a regal nod, rising to her feet, as well. "I had the afternoon free. Paola will see you out."

Holly and Gage turned to leave. Paola had obviously been on standby outside the door, because she appeared in it now.

"Wait." Julia stopped them. Would she finally ask about Kyle, inquire about Holly's profession, her life, perhaps ask her to keep in touch? Holly turned to face her mother again. "Now that you've satisfied your curiosity, I trust this won't be necessary again."

And that was that. "Absolutely unnecessary."

From now on, Julia would be as dead to Holly as Holly obviously was to Julia.

WHAT THE BLOODY HELL had that just been about? It had been the strangest operative contact he'd ever witnessed. Doubt edged in. Could her story have been true?

"If you don't mind, I'd like to return to the hotel," Holly said. Even though she appeared calm, a brittleness surrounded her, as if she'd shatter into a million pieces at the slightest provocation.

"Right. The hotel it is."

"I'd like to take a water taxi, if you can arrange that."

What had happened to her tight budget? Somewhere in that awkward exchange, had she gleaned and/or passed along pertinent information and now she was in a rush to return to the pensione? Or was she genuinely upset? "Certainly."

He arranged the water taxi, mentally running through what had just transpired, searching for any coded messages. He came up blank, unless the name Kyle was some type of code, but that felt like a dead end. At every juncture, the Gorgon wasn't acting as an operative should. She'd had the perfect opportunity to press the attraction between them this morning and seduce him. According to the brief dossier they'd compiled on her, the Gorgon was quick to seduce and use that to her advantage. He mentally shook his head, his instinct giving him a shout-out that things weren't adding up as they should.

A short while later, without the numerous stops of the vaparetto, they were back at the Pensione Armand. Holly had ignored the perfect opportunity to play the sympathy card, which hadn't particularly made sense, considering it would have put him more firmly in her pocket, and had instead kept up an ongoing stream of chatter regarding the various architecture scattered throughout the city.

Gage saw her to her door. Her smile firmly in place, she turned to him. "I'll spend the rest of my day here, if you don't mind. Consider it a free afternoon. Let's say we'll meet downstairs for breakfast tomorrow at eight?"

"I have correspondence and some other things to catch up on so I'll probably stay in my room, too."

"Fine." He noticed the faint tremble of her hands as she unlocked her door. "See you tomorrow." She closed the door in his face.

Within seconds he was in his room and the monitor was up and running. Holly entered the washroom and turned on both sink fixtures wide open. In true operative fashion—preparing to relay information and taking precautions against being overheard—she created a noise distraction. This certainly explained her rush to return. He felt ridiculous that he'd actually considered her story might be true.

But he never expected, never anticipated her next move.

The Gorgon dropped to her knees and retched the contents of her stomach into the loo until apparently there was nothing left.

MOVING IN A STUPOR, Holly brushed her teeth and rinsed with mouthwash. She turned off the faucets and stumbled back into her room, numb with grief.

And that's what it was. Grief.

There'd be no reconciliation, no mother-daughter

bonding, no odd exchange of birthday and Christmas cards. There'd been no begging forgiveness, not even a twinge of remorse, no tell-me-about-you, no let's-keep-in-touch.

Hell, Julia hadn't even called Kyle by name, and she'd introduced her own flesh and blood to her stepdaughter as the daughter of a long-ago acquaintance.

Overhead, a clap of thunder shook the heavens and the roof. As if in commiseration, sudden rain slanted down. With a near-silent keen of mourning, Holly began to cry.

She cried for her motherless childhood, but mostly, she wept for the death of hope. For twenty-seven years there'd always been an unacknowledged glimmer, however faint, that one day all would be revealed and their relationship would mend and become healthy and whole. But it would never happen. She'd seen it today. Never would Julia reach out to her, embrace her, no matter how tentatively. She was nothing to Julia. She had been ever since the day the woman who'd birthed her had walked out the door. It was a harsh realization and her grief gained momentum, welling inside her, seeking release in great, gasping sobs.

She crawled into bed and huddled beneath her covers, pulled the pillow over her head and sobbed for the mother she'd never had and, worst yet, would never have.

A loss of hope was a terrible burden to bear.

GAGE SAT BEFORE THE MONITOR as if turned to stone, unable to look away from the one-woman drama unfolding before him. Emotion—stark, fearsome, debilitating—played out on the screen.

This had nothing to do with an operative exchange.

From a covert standpoint, none of it had made sense. That's because it hadn't been a bloody clandestine meeting. Seasoned, hardened agents such as the Gorgon didn't fall apart afterward like this.

Bugger Mason and bugger the agents who'd identified Holly Smith as the Gorgon and sent him in to ferret out her secrets. He wasn't watching the Gorgon disintegrate into pieces before his very eyes because every instinct he had told him she wasn't the Gorgon. He was watching Holly Smith, a Yank schoolteacher who'd just been crushed by her mother.

He turned off the monitor. Not only should he not be privy to such a private moment, he couldn't watch any longer. He hadn't thought about it in years because the past was done and sitting about ruminating on the maudlin was a monumental waste of time, but he knew, in his gut, in his heart, how Holly Smith felt. Her pain ripped at him.

It hadn't been the day his parents died, nor the day the Colonel had shipped him off to Hempdon's School. No, it had been his first holiday back home. Gage had been so sure a semester of high marks and staying out of trouble, combined with his absence, would make the Colonel fonder of his only grandson. Gage couldn't recall the exact conversation, but he did recall how he'd felt at the precise moment when he realized he'd been chasing a pipe dream. His parents were gone. And even though Gage posed a moral and legal obligation for his grandfather, the Colonel didn't care a whit about him and never would.

He'd lain alone in his magnificent four-poster bed, as befitting the Colonel's sole heir and cried until he could cry no longer.

Gage unfolded himself from the chair and paced the room, current emotion and past pain pursuing him from one wall to the other and back again.

He should ring Mason, report they'd made a monumental bloody mistake, pack his spy toys and return to London. The tour firm could replace him with an authentic guide and Holly's holiday would progress as she'd planned. Clean, neat, simple.

You know what you need to do. His conscience picked a piss-poor time to make an appearance. Holly would be fine. *You're a cad. You witnessed her breakdown. You know how she feels, and you're too cowardly to do what you need to do.*

In his line of work, Gage had killed men. It was one dirty aspect of serving his country. More often than not, it was simply a matter of kill or be killed. He wished he were faced with such a straightforward task now.

He turned on the monitor. Holly remained huddled beneath the covers, a quivering mass.

Bloody, sodding, fucking hell.

He scrubbed his hand through his hair. Life would've been so much easier had she been up and about repairing her face. But then again, life was neither forthright nor easy.

He felt her hurt, her despair, her mourning deep in his soul. He didn't *want* to remember how it felt. He'd been so absolutely alone. *There was no one there for you, but you could be there for her. She needn't be alone now.*

The Gorgon had been his obligation. But Holly Smith wasn't the Gorgon. He'd successfully completed his assignment.

He reached for his case. He'd go ahead and pack. *If you leave her alone, how will you face yourself in the mirror in the morning? You know the door's not locked....*

He left his case and pivoted on his heel. Sod the dog. There was only one way to quiet his nagging conscience.

8

HOLLY DIDN'T HEAR HIM enter. One moment she was in bed alone, and the next, a pair of strong, warm arms wrapped around her and gathered her close. Surprise stemmed her tears.

Gage smoothed her hair back from her damp face and murmured soothingly, "There, there, luv. She's a sodding bitch and certainly not worthy of your tears."

It was all so unexpected—his appearance, his droll delivery, his colorful language. Holly snuffled and laughed.

"I don't know what *sodding* means but it sounds bad, and *bitch* is universal."

"Hold that thought. I'll be back in a flash."

He quickly returned and handed her a wad of toilet tissue. "Blow."

He stepped back out of the room again and she heard running water in the bathroom. While he did whatever he was doing, she blew her nose. He strolled back into the room and her heart flip-flopped at the welcome sight of his broad shoulders, slightly unkempt hair and midnight eyes.

He held a damp washcloth in his hands. "Here, let me tidy you up." He cupped the back of her head in one capable hand and blotted carefully at her face with the other, the cloth cold against her flushed skin. And she knew, soul deep, that he knew how she felt. It wasn't pity. It was empathy. There was a huge difference.

Gooseflesh prickled her skin as he gently blotted the cold cloth against her eyes and temples. "That's cold."

"It's better for the swelling."

"She was awful, wasn't she?" Holly had known it, but it wasn't until she'd actually met Julia that she realized just how different her parents had been. What had her father been thinking?

"Horrid. I'd say you had a lucky escape."

"Escape?"

"What if you'd actually grown up with that narcissistic creature?"

"Oh. I hadn't thought of it that way."

He affected an effeminate shudder, which was quite ridiculous and obviously meant to coax a smile from her because there was nothing remotely effeminate about him. "It's quite remarkable, really, how such a dreadful woman could have such a lovely daughter."

Raw, unwelcome jealousy stabbed her. "That was her stepdaughter."

"Not *her*, you nutter. *You.*"

Oh. "But I look terrible." It wasn't a question. When she cried, her skin got splotchy, her entire nose turned red and her eyes swelled up as if she was suffering an allergic reaction.

Gage stopped blotting at her face and pretended to study her for a moment or two. He nodded his head and shifted the cool cloth to her cheekbone. "Yep. Quite a fright, in fact. Good thing there're no small children about. You'd scatter the little buggers at a glance."

She couldn't seem to help herself—she giggled and swatted at his hand. He feigned surprise. "What? I was just agreeing with you. I thought that was every woman's fantasy—a yes-man. Now, be still so I can restore your normally nonfrightening, thoroughly enchanting visage."

She smiled at his nonsensical chatter but did as he instructed. She absorbed the sensation of his hands against her face, the scent that was uniquely him, the steady rise and fall of his chest before her. "It's not, you know."

"Strictly a matter of opinion. I find your visage eminently enchanting." He brushed the back of his hand along her face.

"I meant the fantasy part. It's not every woman's fantasy to have a yes-man." Despite his teasing, he didn't strike her as a yes-man at all. He seemed very much in control, very much in charge and very much exactly what she wanted.

"You're having me on, right?"

He placed the washcloth on the nightstand.

"You can't do that. It'll ruin the furniture."

"Very well." He stood, rounded the bed and tossed the wet cloth through the bathroom door, onto the tile floor.

He stalked back to the bed, his gaze tangling with hers. She shifted over, making room for him. She should be horrified at how frightful she must look. Instead, the intent in his dark eyes dispelled her reservations and she instead felt very sexy—and very turned on. She'd known they would end up here. She'd known it since their first kiss this morning. Who was she kidding? She'd known it from the moment she'd met him and thought he was the sexiest man who'd ever crossed her path.

Was he her type? Absolutely not. He was too sophisticated. Too sexy. And she wanted him with a fierceness that was new to her. The new, improved Holly could do this. She was going for it. A brief, intense holiday fling.

He sat on the bed's edge and she trembled inside with anticipation.

She'd never looked worse and never felt sexier. "Language is interesting, don't you think? See, you say 'having me on,' and to me, it sounds sort of suggestive, as if you were on me. That's much closer to my idea of a fantasy man."

"I think you may be on to something. Linguistic nuances can be quite fascinating." He cupped her shoulders in his hands, rotating his thumbs in small circles against her shirt. His touch burned through the fabric. "Now, according to your definition, this could be considered having me on."

"Hmm. I suppose. To a degree. We are, after all, discussing nuances."

He wrapped one arm around her waist and hauled her up against him, bending his head as he nuzzled and nibbled at the sensitive juncture of her shoulder and neck, his mouth warm and open against the column of her throat, the underside of her jaw.

She held on to his shoulders and sighed, a slow burn radiating from her thighs throughout her body. "This is getting closer yet to what came to mind, but there are still varying degrees to a nuance."

Gage leaned her back on the bed and moved on top of her, his weight supported by one braced knee. In one smooth motion he raised her hands above her head. Wrapping his hand about her wrists, he kept them in place.

"Is this more of what you had in mind?"

Yes. Definitely. "You're getting there."

He laughed, a low rich sound, and his mouth captured hers. He slid his other free hand beneath her shirt's edge and she moaned into his mouth at the fire that singed her. "More."

He trailed his fingers up her body until he found her breasts. He palmed them through her bra, his tongue exploring the recesses of her mouth, and Holly arched up beneath him. She tugged his shirt free of his pants and smoothed her hands over the muscled ridges of his back. She sucked his tongue into her mouth and he impatiently reached into her bra.

He angled his body over hers, his penis nestling between her thighs, the hard ridge rubbing exquisitely against her. She lifted her hips up, aiming for maximum encounter.

"I…like…the…language you're…speaking," she panted against his mouth.

"It translates even better naked." His breathing was none too steady, either, she noticed.

"Convince me."

"My pleasure."

He whisked her top up over her head and tossed it to the floor. She made equally quick work of his shirt. She'd suspected, she'd thought, she still hadn't imagined… Lean corded muscles defined his broad shoulders, arms, chest and belly. Dark swirls of hair covered his chest and narrowed to an enticing trail leading down to his pants. She reached for his belt at the same time he reached for the waistband of her pants.

"I will if you will," she said.

He levered off of her and the edge of the bed. Then he unbuckled, unzipped, and in one smooth motion divested himself of shoes, socks, pants and briefs.

Long, thick and hard, his blue-veined cock sprang proudly from a nest of dark curls. His sac hung full beneath it. Trim hips gave way to muscular, hair-roughened legs and elegant feet. Her mouth ran dry, quite possibly because all the moisture in her body seemed to have been redirected to between her thighs.

He was intimidatingly, arousingly, damn-near Michelangelo-carved perfect, except he was better hung than David. He leaned down and pulled out a condom from his pocket, placing the foil packet on the nightstand.

Her thighs might be weeping with wanting, but her brain balked at baring herself in front of such perfection. She hadn't brought nearly as good a surprise to show-and-tell as he had. "I don't look like that naked."

He glanced down at his erect penis and then let his hot gaze travel down her. "I should hope not. In fact, I'm counting on it, luv," he drawled. His wicked grin tightened her nipples to taut peaks.

He leaned forward and tugged her pants down over her hips, past her knees, her ankles, over her feet to drop them to the floor.

His grin faded, his eyes darkened, and her breath caught in her throat at the stark appreciation there. His cock quivered. "I want to see all of you." His husky tone, coupled with his obvious appreciation, dispelled her shyness.

She hooked one finger beneath her bra strap and slid it down over her shoulder and then did the same on the other side. He stood, his dark eyes watchful, waiting. She reached behind her, unhooking the bra. As she brought her arms back around, the garment slowly fell away. The hiss of his indrawn breath echoed the downpour of rain outside.

Holly leaned forward and slowly slid her panties down along the same path he'd taken with her pants, letting them fall to the floor at the end of the journey.

A pearl of arousal seeped from the slit of his cock. Emboldened, she leaned back on her elbows, her breasts thrust forward and dropped her legs apart, opening herself to his hot, hungry gaze. Cool air teased her wet slickness.

He murmured something low and arousing in Italian. "You're beautiful." She knew what she looked like, especially after a crying jag, but the reverence in his voice… Even she believed, at that moment, she was a beauty. He traced the bend of her knee with one finger and she felt the light stroke at the core of her being.

Each ply of his fingers against her skin was an awakening, a rebirth. She felt as if she'd never truly been touched until now, until him. Her nerve ends craved and his mouth and hands satiated.

But being touched wasn't enough. She reached between them and smoothed her hands over his chest. She brushed her thumbs over the nubs of his male nipples and she felt him shudder beneath her hands. She plied her fingers through the dark hair on his chest. Finally. A man who looked like a man, acted like a man, smelled like a man and felt like a man. She teased her tongue against the muscled ridge of his shoulder. Hmm. He tasted like a man, as well.

Holly lost track of time because it no longer mattered. Rain lashed against the window and shadows draped the room. Everything got lost in the sensation of his skin against hers, his scent, his taste and the feel of his tongue sweeping the recesses of her mouth, the slide of his hair-roughened leg against hers, the tweaking of her nipples between his fingertips, the heavy thickness and heat of his erection in sweet friction against her dew-slicked folds and her clitoris.

A sweet, hot yearning stole through her body, weighting her limbs, seeping between her thighs. She spread her legs farther, opening herself in invitation. He rolled on the condom, grasped her hips and in one thrust entered her, joining them. He was long and hard and filled her completely. He hooked his arms beneath her knees and set up a slow, steady rhythm, entering her and then nearly withdrawing, long strokes that built momentum inside her until Holly felt the beginning tremors of an orgasm radiate through her.

Gage pistoned harder and faster, his eyes holding her own. Her eyes fluttered closed.

"Look at me," he commanded.

She opened her eyes, her muscles contracting around his hard length as she came and came and came. Long shuddering waves of pleasure overwhelmed her, all the more intense when he came in sync with her. She felt him, knew him, and what should've been just great vacation sex with a sexy foreigner was suddenly something far more intimate.

HOLLY TUGGED A LITTLE MORE of the sheet her way, rolled onto her belly and fixed those amazing eyes on him. He was bloody glad he wasn't required to jump up and chase any bad guys like those poor blokes in action films. He was fairly certain his legs wouldn't support him, and he'd prefer to not fall on his arse. Of course, according to the films, he was supposed to have just slept with her for sport alone and that was disconcertingly not the case.

"What does *sodding* mean?"

Gage rolled to his side to face her, sliding his leg over hers, and tsked. "I can't in good conscience tell you. It's not a term one wants to hear coming from a little Yank with a voice like honey. Leave the British swearing up to me."

Her lips curled in a cheeky smile. "Honey? Really? I thought you probably thought I sounded like a hick."

"No." He'd thought her voice lovely from the beginning. "You sound like a lot of things—warm sun on a cold day, sweet, thick honey. Definitely not a hick."

"Why, thank you, kind sir." She propped her chin in her hand. "I know. It's a derivative of sodomite, isn't it?"

"Clever girl." Tenacious, as well. She didn't let go of things easily.

"Have you ever been to the U.S.?"

"I've made the occasional trip to New York, once to Chicago."

"But you've never visited the South?"

Her line of questioning set off a small alarm. Had he been wrong? "I can't say I've ever had the pleasure." Nor was he planning to soon.

"Well, I'm about to give you an important insider travel tip." He quirked an eyebrow in question. She gave a sensuous little roll that shifted her from her belly to her side. It also afforded him a nice view of her lovely breasts with their honey-hued crests. "There was a little war between the North and the South. Northerners were called Yankees, Southerners were called Rebels. It's been almost a hundred and fifty years, but people tend to have long memories. Calling a Southerner a Yank won't win you any friends if you ever visit the South. It'd be best to leave the term at home."

His alarm quieted. He circled her nipple with a fingertip and it immediately swelled and plumped. Fascinating. "I'll keep that in mind."

He rolled her responsive tip between his thumb and forefinger.

"You're not paying attention to what I'm saying."

He spread his palm over her breast and watched as her nipple peaked through his outspread fingers. "Hmm. Sure I am. Don't call you Johnny Rebs Yanks."

"Gage, I have a question for you."

He was ready to play with her body and all she wanted to do was talk. He bit back a sigh and smoothed his hand down over her side. Okay. They'd talk. For now.

"I'll see what I can do about an answer."

"Why'd you introduce yourself to Julia as my fiancé?"

"Because I'd summed her up in about two seconds and I thought it would put you in a better light, give you a more powerful position than if I was simply there as the hired hand." That was all true. But primarily, he'd done it because it made him seem less of an outsider if it had been, indeed, a meeting between operatives.

He shifted to his back and wrapped his arm around her, pulling her to his side, against his chest, and held her there. She was warm and soft, and her rounded curves fit perfectly against him. She furrowed her fingers into his chest hair and made little patterns.

"Thank you. It made a difference, at least to me. It was nice to have your support."

"Glad I could help. Sorry things turned out the way they did."

"It wasn't really the outcome I wanted. But unfortunately, it wasn't surprising, either. I think I've known all along. But as long as I didn't actually have confirmation, there was hope."

He smoothed his palm up and down her arm, as if he could ease the wound so easily. "It bloody well hurts. And then it makes you wonder what's wrong with you when actually, there's nothing wrong with you at all. They're the ones with the problem."

"Your grandfather?"

He nodded. "Miserable old bastard. And your mother obviously isn't much better than he was." A thought occurred to him. Since Holly wasn't the Gorgon, it put a whole different slant on her actions. "Are you thinking of cutting your trip short since your meeting didn't turn out well?"

"No. Absolutely not. One, I'm not going to run away with my tail tucked between my legs, and second, I'm too cheap. It'd probably cost a fortune to change my ticket." She slid her leg over his and shifted slightly so that she was almost riding his thigh, her full breasts pressed against his side and chest. "Besides, you're already paid for."

A surprised bark of laughter escaped him. "Just paint a scarlet *G* on my head for *gigolo,* would you?"

"I didn't mean it that way. I meant your guide services. But while we're on the subject, do you wind up in bed with your clients often?" She dipped her hand beneath the sheet and slid it across his lower belly, right above his pubic hair. How was he supposed to pay attention with her touching him like that? "I don't have a problem if you do," she said, fingering his navel. Christ, he'd never known that could feel so good. "As far as I'm concerned, what happens in Venice stays in Venice. I'm just curious."

"No. You're the first." He leaned forward and kissed her shoulder, because there was a part of him that couldn't seem to get enough of her touch, her taste, her scent. And questions went both ways. "And you, madam?" She slid her hand down to his thigh and he supposed he'd better do his asking while he could still think. "Do you have affairs with your guides when you travel?"

Holly laughed. "Well, seeing as how this was my first trip, and I'd requested a middle-aged woman who was married as a guide, that answer would be a big, fat no." She gently cupped his scrotum in her hot little hand and did a rolling, squeezing motion that felt so bloody good…. "But after this trip I may take up traveling on a regular basis and make sure I get assigned the sexiest men to show me around."

He laughed but quite honestly, it wasn't that funny. The thought of her lying in bed with another bloke in, say, Prague or Paris with her adept hand wrapped around that guy's balls… Or forget Prague or Paris. What about his replacement here in Venice? "You know, that's poor form, luv, to be talking about the next bloke when you're still in bed with me."

"Oops. Sorry, but you should be flattered. You're setting a very good precedent."

He stared at her for a minute and then laughed. Just when he thought he had her somewhat figured out, she surprised him again. And what she was doing now was near killing him. Ringing the base of his cock with her thumb and finger while she kept her other fingers on his balls, she offered a sliding motion that made her fingers move against his rocks. He moaned aloud. She obviously liked touching him. She rocked against his leg and her core was wet against him. "Let me see if I can make my bad manners up to you."

Perhaps he'd been a bit hasty. It would probably be best if he stuck around for the rest of her trip, just to make sure nothing suspicious happened before he informed Mason that Holly Smith wasn't the Gorgon. After all, he'd already allocated the time in his schedule to be here, so he might as well stick out the remainder of the week.

"Luv, my fault altogether." He slid his hand down her back and delved between her plump cheeks, past her tight rosebud to her juicy folds. "I need to keep you busier so you're not plotting and planning your next tryst."

Her eyes burned bright and hot, and her fingers tightened around his cock when he stroked up her slick flesh to her nubbin. She gasped. "It's raining outside and I didn't buy an umbrella."

He eased two fingers into her tight, hot body, and the unmistakable sound of her juices lapping and sucking at his fingers filled the quiet between them. He chuckled. "Oh, you have an objection to getting wet?"

She wiggled down onto his fingers. "I'm fine with being wet. I'm just not big on the rain."

9

THE NEXT AFTERNOON HOLLY leaned against her room's door frame, extremely tired but also extremely happy.

"So, we'll head out to dinner in say two and a half hours?" Gage said.

"Sure, if that won't make us late for our reservation."

"No. We have ample time. Go ahead, luv, and settle in for a nap." His wicked grin literally curled her toes. "I want you well rested later this evening."

"Ah, typical male. Self-serving rather than genuinely concerned for my health."

"Simply taking care not to ruin the bad reputation of men around the world." He cupped her shoulders in his hands and pressed his lips to her forehead. "Knock if you need me."

He stepped out of her room and she closed the door, melting inside at what she considered a very romantic kiss. He'd known, the same as she'd known, that anything more than that chaste kiss and they'd wind up in bed again. And she was exhausted. Neither of them had gotten much sleep last night and today had been busy, but altogether wonderful.

Holly fell back onto her bed, replaying the last few hours in her mind. They'd held hands and strolled among the markets bursting with fresh, ripe fruits and succulent fresh vegetables, past small shops with mouthwatering pastries displayed in the windows. She'd admired the remarkable workmanship behind the lace and masks and glassware all produced by Venetian artisans.

And neither one of them had been able to keep their hands off of the other, whether it was holding hands or just a feathering of fingers against the other's shoulders. Or her arm around his waist and his arm slung around her shoulder. And she, who had never been given to public displays of affection, had discovered a shameless aspect of her character.

Given her terrible sense of direction, she'd had no idea where they'd strayed, but it had been an older part of what was a very old city. A narrow alley, no wider than two people, ran between two buildings connected far above by stone arches. They'd slowed and finally stopped, halfway down the shadowed alley, and kissed.

Fanned by a morning of touching and promising glances, they'd both quickly gone up in flames. Gage had pinned her against the rugged brick wall with his hard body. While their tongues tangled, he'd slid his hand beneath her shirt and palmed her breasts, his fingers tweaking and plucking at her nipples.

She had nearly come then and there, excited by the knowledge that at any moment they could be discovered. She had wanted him with a careless, wanton fierceness that still shocked her and left her trembling. She'd wanted him to take her there, then, against the wall in that alleyway. And if she'd had on a dress with an easily lifted hem… But the concept lost its erotic edge at the idea of tugging down slacks.

She'd been beyond aroused by the alleyway encounter and he'd known it. She'd seen the knowledge in those dark eyes of his. It was as if she and Gage were tuned into the same frequency. Several times throughout the day, they'd communicated with just a look. There'd been times she'd guessed what he was going to say before he said it.

And she was more aware than ever of some brooding secret he kept, something she felt sure that tied into her. But at this point, she wanted him, secrets and all.

She'd felt an incredible, overwhelming attraction the first moment she'd set eyes on Gage Carswell. An affair with him also helped ease Julia's rejection and kept her from thinking about it. Who needed therapy?

She hadn't called her father yet. Yesterday, she'd felt too raw to hear him say "I told you so." He'd been adamant against her coming. This morning, with the time difference, it'd been too early to call. And she'd been otherwise occupied with Gage in an activity that didn't lend itself to making her think of calling her father.

She rolled to her side and dug out her cell phone. Time to get it over with, then she could nap in peace.

Her dad answered on the third ring. Holly suddenly wanted to buy a little more time. She also wanted to know about her cat.

"Hey, Daddy. How's Ming getting along at your house?"

"He's fine. It's the damnedest thing. He and Gidget have taken a shine to each other."

"What?" Gidget, Marcia's apricot toy poodle, pretty much disliked everyone except for Daddy and Marcia. The plan had been to keep Gidget and Ming separated. "How'd that happen?"

"I told you it was the damnedest thing. Ming escaped—"

"I warned you he was sneaky."

"You were right. I didn't even know he'd gotten out of the bedroom we'd set up for him. I came in to watch TV and there they were, him and Gidget curled up together in her dog bed. They've been joined at the hip ever since."

"At least he's not pining for me." She'd been concerned about leaving her pet alone. Abandoned by a family moving to Kansas who hadn't bothered to move him, too, Ming had come to Holly from a cat-rescue group. The last thing she'd wanted was for him to think she'd left him behind, too. Who cared whether the toy poodle liked Holly, as long as she'd made Ming feel welcome. "I'll have to buy Gidget some treats when I get back."

"She's partial to the liver-flavored ones." Holly could hear the smiling indulgence in her father's voice.

"Then I'll make sure I get her those." She drew a deep breath. "I met Julia yesterday."

Her father's tension was a palpable force on the other end. "How was she?"

"A bitch." Holly really hadn't planned to say it. It just came out. But it was the truth, so she left it.

"I'm sorry, honey. I was afraid, but I'd hoped for your sake. I'm sorry, baby. I knew we weren't the same type of people, but I loved her and I thought that would be enough. I made a mistake all those years ago and you and Kyle, especially you, have paid for it."

"Daddy, I'm fine. Truly, I am." And she realized, she was. It still hurt, but it wasn't agonizing. Gage had nailed Julia when he'd pegged her as a narcissist. Julia had the problem, not Holly. And in a sudden insight, she realized she was incredibly lucky. However difficult parts of the past twenty-seven years had been *without* Julia, they would have been far worse *with* her. "I think her leaving was a close call for all of us."

There was a long pause on the other end of the line. And then he asked the question, as if it were being dragged out of him, as if he didn't want to ask but simply couldn't stop himself. "Did she ask about me?"

Holly closed her eyes to the pain behind the naked longing in that one awful question. He was her dad and she loved him. For all his faults, he'd been a good father and tried to give her enough love to make up for her missing mother. She wanted to tell him what he obviously so desperately wanted to hear. But she couldn't give him a lie. She knew he loved Marcia. And Marcia deserved all of him, not Julia's leftovers.

"No. She didn't ask about you. She didn't ask about Kyle. She didn't ask about any of us. She only had two questions. She asked me why I was there, and when I started to leave, she asked me if it would be necessary for me to see her again."

It was harsh and comfortless, but the truth often was. "Let her go, Dad. She's not worth another passing thought from any of us." Unfortunately love didn't appear to be doled out based on merit.

"I wish you'd never gone." His voice held an edge of bleak anger.

She refused to be shot as the messenger. "I'm not. I'm glad I came. I have no regrets." Even though she'd felt devastated yesterday, she didn't regret finding and confronting Julia. It was done. It was closure—ugly closure—

but closure nonetheless. She'd initiated it, driven it. She owned her closure.

Her father sighed on the other end. "How's that tour guide that Josephine set you up with working out?"

Her cousin hadn't technically set her up with the tour guide, she'd merely recommended them, but Holly wasn't splitting hairs. "Fine."

"Is she a pretty nice lady, the one showing you around?"

Now, on the heels of the Julia letdown, didn't seem the best time to get into the guide-switch situation. "My guide is very nice and very knowledgeable." About lots of things.

"That's good."

"I'm having a wonderful time. Today was incredible. I'm going to go now so I can get in a nap before dinner. I won't call any more until my flight gets in on Saturday if that's okay."

"That's fine. I love you, Holly-berry."

Pulling out her nickname was his way of apologizing for his earlier flash of anger. "I love you, too, Daddy. Now, go tell your wife you love her."

"You're a smart girl. I think I will."

She ended the call and rolled onto her side, bunching the pillow under her head. She felt as if a two-ton gorilla, if there was such a thing, had jumped off her back.

Her eyes drifted closed and she fell asleep thinking about Gage.

The Gorgon blinked, just when she almost had the amber-tinted contact lens in place. "Dammit."

Millions of people wore contact lenses every day. How hard could it be to put them in? She centered the lens on her finger and pulled her right eye open one more time, determinedly seating it over her pupil. There. She closed her eyes the way the woman in the optical department had instructed and let it settle into place.

She opened them and stared at herself in the mirror. Instead of her striking aqua eyes, she now had amber eyes that went with her new honey-blond hair. She hated disguising her eyes this way. She carefully removed the loathsome contacts, put them in their container and placed it with her airline ticket, impatience rippling through her.

Steady. She calmed herself. Years of patience and careful planning had gotten her this far. She couldn't discount that luck and opportunity had been handed to her in this instance, but both were useless if one wasn't prepared to act on them. She, being the incomparable Gorgon, had seized her opportunity.

She'd known she would have to retire soon. She was becoming too well-known and a well-known agent was a dead agent. She'd calculated she had one good exchange left before she was forced to retire. And then opportunity had knocked. This was a beautiful thing. Holly, while on her trip to Venice to find her bitch of a mother, would deliver the package in three days. The money would be wired to the Gorgon's offshore account, Holly would be terminated, and in the international spy community, it would become known that the Gorgon had met her end, leaving the true Gorgon free to enjoy the spoils of her labors. And it was about time. Life had dealt her a lousy hand, but she'd persevered and soon she'd have the life she deserved, the life she'd been denied.

She already had a plastic surgeon lined up for next week. A nose job, cheek and chin implants, a brow lift, collagen lips, liposuction for her waist and thighs and a new set of breasts and she would finally be the woman she was destined to be. She'd known since she was a small child that she was special. Her eyes had told her. Soon the rest of her would match her eyes.

Her cell phone trilled. It was him. Her lip curled in disdain. He was ostensibly calling with his update, but she knew it was really just so she could reassure him—again—and get him off. She'd get whatever information he had for her just as soon as she talked him through a jack-off session.

He was so needy, but he'd been so useful. She'd invested months in researching and putting together a list of men in positions that would prove helpful and then she'd looked for the most vulnerable on the list. He'd won the prize. She'd put up with his superciliousness, his constant need for assurance and his rather inept sexual performances—which she nonetheless lauded as spectacular—and it was paying off. He kept her informed, and she kept him satisfied but just needy enough that he came back to her for more.

She deliberately waited until the call was about to go to voice mail before she answered. She knew just how to push his buttons and make him frantic, thinking she might be with someone else. She fed his insecurity and paranoia. It was all the more powerful when she lied that no one else had ever satisfied her the way he did.

"Are you alone?"

She smiled. "Of course." She wouldn't be later, but she was now. "And lonely. Waiting on you to call," she said, interjecting a pouting note.

"Now that I have, what shall we talk about?"

That was her cue to start the phone sex. She'd discovered his lack of sexual imagination early on. No oral sex. No anal sex. No doggie-style. None of the things she really liked. He wanted to hear the same thing every time, a description of the two of them in a bed, in the dark, in the missionary position with her constantly complimenting his body, his size, his technique. Any deviation from the *script* and he wasn't happy. She settled back on the bed and reached for her dildo with the hummingbird that would massage her clit once she inserted the main shaft.

She spread her legs and flipped the on switch. She didn't believe in faking an orgasm. It didn't seem honest and she deserved better.

"WE RAN EVERYONE AT THAT address and they were all clean," Mason said, his displeasure evident in his clipped tones. "Another dead end."

Gage wasn't surprised Julia's address had yielded nothing, because he now knew that meeting had been precisely what it seemed. Holly Smith wasn't the Gorgon and he had shared that with Mason. He was paid to relay verifiable information he discerned through surveillance, but he couldn't ignore gut instinct. And since this was supposed to be a watch-and-observe operation, Holly shouldn't be in any danger. But the question begged asking—where, then, was the real Gorgon? Was she, too, in Venice? Had they missed her? Or was Holly Smith simply a red herring and the impending deal would take place in another city?

And still there was another piece of the puzzle that didn't quite fit. He hadn't heard the slightest rumblings that an important deal was about to go down. "How reliable was the source that reported something substantial impending?" Gage inquired.

"A stringer I've used before."

Unlike Gage, who was given assignments to complete, stringers were more along the lines of informants who approached the handlers and were paid for bits of information. It was in a stringer's best interest long-term to only sell solid information. A few rounds of collecting a fee for bad information and a stringer might soon find themselves without a buyer.

"Was it verified?" Often if a stringer's information had a big impact, it would carry a bigger price tag. Something substantial impending certainly qualified and so Mason had probably checked with other agencies to authenticate the information. In fact, on Gage's last assignment, he'd discovered news outside his jurisdiction regarding a black-market organ-donor operation fetching millions of pounds a year. He'd lucked into names of doctors and suppliers. Quite a nice bit of information to stumble upon and quite a dirty lot to put out of business. Had Gage been a stringer, that information would've fetched quite a sum. As it stood, it had simply been a bonus in his final report. In this case, however, he was sure Mason would've verified through the CIA and perhaps even the French.

"Of course I did," Mason snapped.

Curious, that. There'd been no tail, no other spooks since he'd arrived. He was sure of it. He'd wager, at the least, a few of those CIA blokes should've been sniffing about. She was, after all, American, and they had a rather large stake in this, too. In his experience, the CIA chaps, even the clandestine ones, were a rather obvious lot at best. If they were here and had Holly under surveillance, he'd have seen them. Quite curious, indeed.

"I'll call tomorrow afternoon with an update."

"See that you do. In the meantime, carry on."

Mason hung up and Gage paced to the window overlooking the curving street. Everything appeared to be right in the world, which was, in itself, quite worrisome. The instinct that had kept him alive for a decade in this business said all was not as it appeared.

"THIS IS FANTASTIC," Holly said.

The waiter seated them and Gage watched the almost-childlike wonder and excitement on Holly's face when she realized their table gave them a splendid view of Venice by night.

It was the same expression he'd noted their first morning together while en route to Coin, the same excitement he'd seen in her all day and yesterday. He loved watching her. She was like a breath of fresh air compared to other women he knew, ones who wore jaded sophistication as if it were the latest accessory.

And he liked making her smile, whether it was strolling along the Fondamenta della Sensa or her flying apart in his arms as he made love to her. Before Holly, he'd known a hollow contentment. Now he realized a very subtle distinction. Contentment wasn't happiness. Happiness hadn't been in his vocabulary. Somewhere along the way, he'd arrived at the subconscious conclusion that there were people in life who weren't slated for happiness. But it was the oddest bloody thing—he'd discovered Holly's happiness brought him a cautious joy. It was quite the novel experience.

"I thought you would like it."

The restaurant was elegant, yet not pretentious. The tables along the walls were very similar to an opera box, enclosed on three sides, the fourth side open, leaving them with the view. Rather than chairs, banquettes upholstered in rich leather lined the three walls, the high-end equivalent of a booth. Pristine white linens draped the tables to the floor. Securing a "boxed" table had cost him a small fortune.

Classical Italian music mingled with the clink of silverware and the hum of conversation, forming a backdrop of sound. Murano glass wall sconces and tabletop candles provided low, muted light.

Gage ordered a bottle of Prosecco, the Veneto's own sparkling wine, and polenta, grilled radicchio, a fish soup flavored with saffron and eels prepared with tomato sauce, white wine and garlic. At Holly's request, they were all traditional Venetian dishes and he lauded her willingness to sample them, especially the eel.

The steward delivered and served the Prosecco and *finally* they were alone. Rather than sitting across from each other, they sat side by side, ostensibly so they could both enjoy the drama of the Grand Canal and the buildings lining it, visible through the window. He raised his glass to Holly's. "To time spent in Venice."

"To time spent in Venice." She echoed his sentiment and touched her glass to his. They both drank, but neither looked away from the other.

She wore the dress she'd purchased at Coin. Her eyes appeared luminous above the sworls of blue and green in the dress. The fabric clung lovingly to the fullness of her breasts and the curve of her shoulders, offering a tantalizing hint of cleavage. She'd loosely pinned her hair up and back, leaving her lovely neck bare, with tendrils framing her face.

"You are quite lovely tonight." She enchanted him.

"You could have any woman in this room. Several, in fact, have let you know that since we arrived."

"There are other women here? Really? I hadn't noticed." And he quite honestly hadn't, outside of a quick scan for anyone who looked like another operative.

"You're having me on, Gage Carswell," she said in that soft Southern drawl.

"I assure you, luv, you're the only woman I want. And make no mistake that I do want you." He wanted her the way she'd been earlier today in the alley. Carnal inspiration struck him. He casually reached beneath the white-linen-draped table and stroked her leg. "And when we get back to the hotel, I plan to lick and suck and taste every inch of you. But I'm not sure that I can wait that long." He slid his hand higher to the soft inside of her knee and her breath hitched in her throat. "The washroom's just around the corner. Go slip off your knickers, luv."

"Now?"

"Now."

"But—" Her eyes glittered and she moistened her lush lower lip with the tip of her tongue.

"You know you want to. Remember, luv, I was there with you in the alley today. No one will know you're deliciously bare except you and me."

Her eyes were already changing to a hue more green than blue, a sure sign of her excitement. She placed her napkin on the table. "If you'll excuse me."

He stood along with her and caught her wrist in his hand. Her pulse fluttered wildly beneath his fingertips. "Don't start without me."

Her smile was pure seduction. "I'll try."

10

HIS GAZE BURNED AGAINST her back as she crossed the room. The bathroom sat tucked in a small hallway to the left of the dining room. She locked the door behind her and her belly quivered with excitement. As a rule, she never went commando, but she found the idea daring and incredibly arousing. Life was short. She had three more days in a city she'd probably never return to with a man she wouldn't see again. If he wanted her without panties, then she'd go without panties.

She slipped off the already-damp underwear. Amazing what a difference a scrap of fabric made. Without it, she felt wild and sexy and abandoned. And even though he'd suggested it, it still felt more proactive than reactive, she mused as she rolled the panties up and shoved them in her purse. She did a quick mirror check. Venice agreed with her. She wasn't being vain—she looked good. Her eyes sparkled and she couldn't seem to stop smiling. She looked like a woman with a satisfying lover. Who was she kidding? Gage was what agreed with her.

She was incredibly aware of her own bareness, the slight friction of skin against skin between her thighs as she crossed the room.

He rose when she returned, and once again she was

struck by what she considered his courtliness. Men she knew didn't stand when a woman left or returned to the table. She liked it.

He didn't mention it. She didn't mention it. But they both *knew*. Even the dinner napkin laid across her lap felt erotic.

They sipped the semidry sparkling wine and discussed the following day's itinerary, her final tour of Venice, which included the famed Campanile, Doge's Palace and Basilica San Marco in the morning and, if weather permitted, a quick lagoon hop to Murano in the afternoon.

A current of anticipation ran beneath the desultory conversation, charging the air between them. She deliberately didn't mention her trip to the restroom. If he wanted to know if she'd done what he'd requested, he'd have to ask. Wasn't he going to say anything? Do anything? He'd been careful not to even touch her since she'd returned to the table.

"Did you do what I asked?" His dark eyes intense, he looked at her over the rim of his wineglass.

"Yes." Energy, tension, awareness pulsed between them.

He raised the glass to his lips. "Show me."

"They're in my purse." She deliberately misunderstood and reached to her left, where she'd placed her bag on the seat next to her.

"No. Show me. You've got your napkin in your lap. Slide your dress up and let me see."

Well, that was a different showing altogether. Beneath the cover of her white linen napkin, Holly slid the dress up her legs, past her thighs. She left her napkin in place and gazed at him innocently. He was issuing commands, but she was ultimately in charge. When she'd boarded that plane, when she'd tracked down Julia, when she'd made the decision to take this man as her lover, she'd left behind the uncertainty that had plagued her in relationships, in sex, in life.

"Move your napkin, luv."

Much as in the alleyway today, the idea of being in an upscale restaurant where their waiter could return at any moment was…exciting. Almost as exciting as the heated glint in Gage's dark eyes.

She lifted the napkin to blot at her lips and watched him watch her. She felt the sizzle of his gaze between her thighs. His face tightened, his nostrils pinched and his eyes grew heavy-lidded.

"Spread your legs." His voice was low and hoarse.

"But that's not ladylike," she said, feigning shock.

"I know." He didn't have to feign his wicked look.

She spread her legs, her knee nudging his. She was open, exposed, and almost unbearably aroused.

"Christ…"

Another sip of wine and she emptied her glass.

"Look at yourself."

Well, she'd deliberately avoided doing just that, pretty sure that her thighs weren't nearly as toned as they should be. But suddenly, it really didn't matter if they were a little heavier than she liked because Gage seemed very, very turned on by her, un-toned thighs and all.

She looked down. She was all-white thighs, dark curls and a hint of pink. Arousing. Erotic.

"More wine?"

"Please."

"Are you wet?"

"Yes."

"How wet?"

"Very." She looked at his fingers wrapped around the delicate stem of the wineglass. She loved his hands and ached for the touch of his fingers against her. "You could check for yourself."

"I could, couldn't I?" he asked, but he made no move to touch her.

Ah, two could play at this game. She glanced at his crotch. She thought she detected a tad of tenting, but it was difficult to tell with his napkin draped across his thighs. "Are you hard?"

It wasn't her imagination—his napkin actually moved. If he hadn't been hard before, he was now. She suspected, however, that he'd just become harder. She leaned into him and murmured into his ear, "Are your balls tight?"

She draped the napkin back over her lap.

"Vixen."

"Tease."

Excellent timing on her part as the waiter arrived with their appetizer. "You are both hungry, no?"

"Ravenous," Gage said.

"Ah, you will enjoy the polenta. It is *delicioso*. Another bottle of wine, *signore?*"

"Yes."

Holly picked up a piece of the polenta and held it to Gage's mouth. "Since you're ravenous."

His lips closed around her, his tongue lapping at her fingertips. Even the way the man chewed was sensual— slow and thorough. She watched the column of his throat work as he swallowed.

"It's good, but it could be better. You know what I want."

"What happened to not starting without you?"

"You're not. I'm right here."

Holly reached beneath the napkin and the edge of her dress and slid two fingers into her wet heat. Bringing her hand back up, her fingers glistened in the candle-light.

She plucked a small piece off of the serving plate and, once again, brought it to Gage's lips. The musky scent of her feminine arousal hung between them. He took her fingers into his mouth and repeated that erotic lapping with his tongue.

Holly could barely breathe.

"Superb. Nothing has ever tasted that good. I've seen you, smelled you, heard you, tasted you, *now* I'm going to touch you."

Yes. Finally. She opened her legs farther, ready, willing, waiting…. Gage placed his hand on her knee and she quivered. God, could she stand this?

"Your wine, *signore, signora.* Shall I open it?"

"Yes, please."

Holly was acutely aware of Gage's hand on her knee and her splayed legs while Pietro poured the wine. He topped off their glasses and picked up the empty bottle from the tabletop. "Everything is to your liking?"

Gage curled his fingers around her knee. "Perfect."

Pietro nodded as he backed away. "Enjoy."

Before Pietro had disappeared, Gage dragged her knee over the top of his, leaving her gapingly open beneath the napkin and the tablecloth's edge.

"I don't care who comes to the table," Holly murmured against his ear, her pearled nipple grazing his arm. "Don't stop this time."

"You want me to touch you?" He slid his hand higher up her leg.

"Yes." She fought the urge to drop her head back and close her eyes. Instead she raised her wineglass to her lips.

He caressed her inner thigh and wanting shivered through her all the way to her womb. "Like this?"

"More." She sipped from the glass.

"What about this?" He threaded one finger through her drenched curls and lightly traced along the outside of her mound.

She forced herself to remain still and not buck her hips toward his elusive finger. He stroked down the outside of her, not actually touching the eager, hungry nerve endings found farther in. If he didn't touch her, *really* touch her soon, she'd scream. She didn't care if they were in a restaurant, she didn't care about anything but the burning, driving craving to have his finger between her thighs stroking her, touching her in that place that throbbed for him.

And then he swiped his long, blunt-tipped finger along her honeyed channel. How she didn't cry out would forever remain a mystery to her. Instead, she whimpered.

"Oh, Holly." He circled her intimate lips with his fingertip. "You're so, so wet, luv."

Slowly, he slid a finger into her tight channel and Holly bit her lower lip to keep from crying out at the feeling of pleasure and the mounting need that plagued her. Gage slid back out of her and then in again, this time inserting two fingers. She clenched around him and brought her knees together, trying to force him deeper.

He withdrew his hand and reached for his wineglass. She gasped. "You can't—"

He curled his fingers around the wine stem. "Ah, but I can." He drank.

Well, this was a fine mess she was in. Her wicked lover had her literally weeping for his touch. She reached for her napkin and realized that somewhere along the way it'd fallen off of her lap. She shifted the tablecloth a bit and spotted it. It was caught in the folds of the tablecloth. She bent lower….

"What're you doing?"

"I've dropped my napkin. I've almost got it." She leaned farther down but everything shifted and the napkin dropped to the floor. Holly turned her head slightly and realized her face was nearly in Gage's lap. And Gage's lap, even with the cover of his napkin, was sporting one heck of an erection.

There was no great internal debate. There wasn't even a real conscious thought process on her part. It was nothing more and nothing less than feminine sexual instinct. One minute she was leaning down, the next she slipped beneath the table.

"HOLLY?"

She grabbed the napkin and placed it on the floor in front of Gage's legs. "I dropped my napkin," she whispered back. Did she dare? The old Holly, the unsure Holly would climb back out and spend the rest of the evening thinking about what she wished she'd done.

Not this time.

"We'll get you another—"

She angled herself between his legs, kneeling on the napkin, and slid her hands up his thighs. His voice died midsentence. She smiled to herself as she smoothed her hand over his crotch and the hard, straining ridge of his penis. "Slide forward," she stage-whispered.

"Luv…" he protested. But still, he slid. She eased his zipper down, mindful of the press of his erection against his pants, and then reached inside and freed him. Even though she was no stranger to his body, his erect penis loomed even larger in the confines beneath the table. Her entire body quivered in anticipation.

She stroked up one side of him with her finger, rimmed the head and back down the ridge that ran along the underside of his erection. She felt the rush of blood beneath the velvety skin, the flow of energy between them. His male scent called to her.

She cupped his sac in her hand, rolling him against her palm, and didn't miss the hissed intake of his breath. Her own heartbeat rushed inside her chest, fueled by the smell, the sight, the feel of him.

Even in the near-darkness beneath the table, she could see he was gorgeous. She wrapped her hand around his shaft and stroked up and down, feeling the velvet skin give and take. She canted her head to the side and slid her tongue up his sensitive ridge until she reached the top, where she slowly licked around the outer part of his crown. Between her thighs, her muscles constricted reflexively at the taste of him. She lapped at his slit, capturing a drop of his salty essence on the tip of her tongue, and she knew there was no going back.

She took him in her mouth, loving the hard length of him filling her mouth, the musky scent of his masculine arousal. Her own juices ran down her thighs as she sucked on his cock, sheltered from the restaurant by the floor-length tablecloth.

"Your dinner, *signore*." She stilled, his length still in her mouth, at the sound of Pietro's voice from above.

She really shouldn't… She should wait… They were likely to be discovered if she didn't.

She didn't wait.

She filtered out the conversation and once again slid her mouth up and down his magnificent cock, her hand stroking his base in rhythm with her mouth while she wrapped his balls in her other hand.

It was tight, close quarters, but it merely added to her excitement. He didn't dare buck his hips or call her name. He had to stay still as she worked her mouth up and down his shaft. His balls tightened in her hand, his thighs tensed tighter and tighter against her shoulder until his salty essence filled her mouth. She came close to finding her own shuddering release with his.

She tucked him back into his pants and zipped him back up. She cautiously raised the tablecloth. "Is anyone looking?"

"Only the entire establishment." What… "No. No one's looking."

She slid back into her spot.

"Bloody hell, Holly. That was…"

"My appetizer. And here I see the main course has arrived." He still looked rather dazed. "Do you think you could arrange a fresh napkin for me? I seem to have misplaced mine."

11

"I HAVE A SURPRISE FOR YOU," Gage said, checking his watch as they left the restaurant. Excellent. Right on time.

It wasn't nearly the surprise she'd given him earlier. He'd thought it bloody inspired when he'd asked her to lose her knickers, but then again Holly was altogether an inspiring woman. But his imagination was absolutely nothing compared to hers.

She linked her arm through his, leaning into him. "I know what I'd like as a surprise."

He chuckled. "Lusty wench," he said, in an unusually playful mood, brought about, no doubt, by the unexpected treat she'd given him. The rest of the meal had been incredible, as if his senses had been at their highest awareness. He reminded himself she hadn't enjoyed the release he had. But he'd take care of that...

"Where I'm from, a winch is something used to haul a tractor out of the mud."

He led her down the steps to the quay, having once again ascertained that they hadn't picked up a tail from the restaurant. "Ah, that cultural difference again." He bowed from the waist. "Your gondola awaits you, fair maiden."

She shook her head. "Wait. How'd I go from being a lusty wench to a fair maiden?"

He stepped closer to her warmth, the night air ruffling her hair against her cheek. "Perhaps because you're enchantingly both." Dipping his head and pressing a kiss against her brow, he tucked her hair behind her ear and let his fingers linger against the delicate shell.

She tilted her head to one side, glancing up at him from beneath her lashes. "Enchanting? Really?"

Laughing, he wrapped his arm around her waist and turned her to the row of black boats standing ready. "Stop wheedling for compliments. Your gondola is ready." It hadn't been listed on her itinerary. He suspected it was yet another case of her pinching her pennies.

She tried to back up, but only pressed herself more firmly against his arm around her waist. "It was a really thoughtful gesture but I, um, don't want to ride in a gondola."

"Why ever not?" It had to be the money issue. "Don't worry about the expense. This is my treat. Something I wanted to do for you."

"That's so sweet but I really can't," she said, slipping free of his embrace.

Gage nearly choked. He couldn't recall that anyone had ever referred to him as sweet. "They're perfectly safe."

"It's not the safety issue." She wrapped her arms around her middle, looking decidedly uncomfortable. "Um, I know it's kind of quirky, but…it's the germs."

"Germs?"

"Well, yeah. I sort of have this thing about germs. The water taxis and the vaporetti all sit higher in the water. But the gondolas are just right there, at the water line, and God knows what's in that canal."

The careful inspection of the bathroom, the furtive examination of cutlery and serving pieces before she dined all made sense now. What didn't fit, however, was what had happened earlier at dinner. Once again, he wrapped his arm around her waist and gathered her close. He leaned down and murmured in her ear. "Luv, pardon my bluntness, but you just crawled beneath a restaurant table and made me a very happy bloke. Now you're concerned you might encounter a drop of canal water?"

"I know. I— That was just— I was caught up in the moment. You'd been touching me and then I leaned down to grab my napkin and *it* was right there and I was so wound up I didn't really stop to think. But I did spread the napkin on the floor."

Knowing she had been so turned on she'd forgotten her phobia, that was a cock-rush.

He trailed a path of small kisses down her neck, her skin slightly chilled in the early spring night. "You can't leave Venice without a gondola ride." He slipped off his dinner jacket and wrapped it around her shoulders. She snuggled into it and leaned against him.

"Won't you be cold?"

"No. There's a nice warm lap blanket in the gondola, and I'll make sure you won't come into contact with the water. Our gondolier wouldn't have a job for very long if he allowed his patrons to get wet. It's a tradition that's passed down from generation to generation, a position of great pride."

"You really want to go in that gondola don't you?"

He hadn't forgotten her earlier joke about taking up with more guides. He was resolute—whatever experiences followed for her, none would touch Venice.

"No. I really want to go in that gondola with *you*."

"Okay," she relented, tugging his jacket more tightly around her. "Let's complete my Venetian experience."

Her enthusiasm wasn't exactly overwhelming, but once she realized she wasn't going to come into contact with any canal germs, she'd enjoy it.

He and the gondolier, Alberto, handed her into the boat carefully. While she'd napped this afternoon, Gage had popped out to select a boat and arrange the time. He'd thought this vessel particularly elegant.

By law, all gondolas were painted black, but some were more lavish than others. The seat in this boat was well padded and upholstered in a rich cream and blue with a thick fringe trim on the edges. An ornate polished brass shell and scroll design decorated the back. Brass *trevisian,* or sea horses, cast locally, embellished the sides. He'd found it regal and opulent yet tasteful.

Gage settled on the seat beside her, her hip and thigh pressing against his, and arranged the blanket over their laps. Alberto poled them away from the quay, and Gage instructed him in Italian to take the longest route possible through some of the smaller side canals.

He put his left arm around Holly's shoulders and she fit against his side like a jigsaw piece. Unfortunately, she was tense. He felt it in her body's rigidness, saw it in the slight pinching of her profile etched against the Venetian background. That simply wouldn't do.

He spent the next few minutes pointing out palaces, relaying their histories, and gradually the tension seeped out of her.

She sighed and leaned her head against his shoulder. "Hmm. You were right. This is beautiful."

From the stern, Alberto began to sing, a low, soft

baritone, more as if he was singing for himself than them. The high back of the seat and the brass ornamentation afforded them a measure of privacy. They sat, gliding through the water, encapsulated in their own world.

Gage strummed the softly sculpted line of her jaw with his fingers, turning her head to him. He brushed his lips against hers, relishing the feel, the scent of her against his mouth. He slanted his head and kissed her, slowly, thoroughly until her mouth blossomed open beneath his and her tongue met his. She drove him mad.

"I think I just transitioned from fair maiden to lusty wench," she murmured against his mouth.

"I believe you're correct. Are your knickers still in your purse?"

"My memory suddenly seems very faulty. Perhaps you'd better check."

"What a smashing idea." He kissed her again and under the cover of the night and the blanket across their laps, he slid his hand up her damp inner thigh and brushed one finger along her curls. She was drenched.

She issued a small sound of entreaty in the back of her throat and slid her arm around his back, angling her body more into his. With her face pressed against his neck, he fingered her slick full nether lips. Her core was wet and hot. He found the sweet nubbin at the top and slathered her nectar over it.

He inserted one finger into her channel and she tightened around him. He slowly drew it out, her honey coating him. A second finger joined the first and once again she gripped him. He found her clit with his thumb and then proceeded to play with her—stroking, teasing, sliding two fingers in and out of her while he thumbed her clit, and just when she was about to come, he'd withdraw his fingers and start all over again, knowing she couldn't cry out, couldn't make him give her what she wanted while the gondolier poled the boat forward.

"Remember when I had to carry on a conversation with the waiter while you had my cock in your mouth?"

"Yes." Her answer was muffled against his neck.

"Look over your shoulder and ask Alberto how long he's been doing this. Ask him to tell you about his boat. And then ask him to sing something special for you."

Her breath was uneven. "Won't he know?"

"That depends on you."

He turned with her, ostensibly to participate in the conversation, but actually, he wanted to watch her face.

Holly smiled at Alberto and started talking while he began his ministrations once again. Stroking, petting, plucking, plunging. And she was incredibly, undeniably turned on. Her excitement was evidenced by just how wet she was and getting wetter by the minute.

"You have a lovely—" did Alberto notice how her breath caught on that word as Gage stroked his finger against her sensitive inner wall, high inside her? "—voice. Would you mind singing for us again?"

Alberto laughed and launched into another low, soulful serenade. He seemed much more wrapped up in the role he was playing than in the couple in front of him, which suited Gage just fine.

"Not only are you a lusty wench, you're a naughty one, as well. You enjoyed talking to Alberto while I diddled you beneath the blanket, didn't you?"

A streetlight they floated past illuminated her glimmering eyes. "No. I didn't like it at all."

"Naughty and lying. I think I'll have to punish you. Maybe I'll just leave you this way."

She clamped her thighs around his hand to hold him in place. "Don't you dare. Yes, I liked it. I loved it. Now, please…" Her mouth latched on to his and she pulled his tongue into her mouth, sucking it and stroking it the same way she'd done earlier to his cock.

With the evidence of her desire lapping at his fingers, he slid in and out of her silken channel some more, rotating his thumb against her swollen clit. Her body tensed against him, and he swallowed her muffled cry as her orgasm rained against his hand.

"Oh, Gage…"

He kept his hand inside her. She was so aroused, so responsive. But they weren't done yet.

He called over his shoulder to Alberto. "Bravo. One more, please." He looked into Holly's heavy-lidded eyes. "And you, too, luv. One more."

"I can't…."

He massaged that spot high inside her inner wall and she leaned farther into him, her mouth finding his. "Well, maybe I can," she murmured as he stroked her into another orgasm.

HOLLY COULD BARELY LIFT her head off of Gage's shoulder. Multiple orgasms had never happened for her. Or was it considered a back-to-backer? Either way, it was a totally new experience. In fact, she'd been so incredibly ready, so turned on, she'd felt as if she might die if she didn't come… And then he'd done it all over again. Send Gage Carswell to the head of the class. She felt as if she'd just had an out-of-body experience.

He was warm and it was so comfortable melting against him in the aftermath of *that*. A slight breeze shifted her hair and Gage reached up to smooth it off his jaw. Her intimate scent clung to his hand.

She looked up at the light shining in one of the upper windows of a private residence. "It must be odd to live in a place where there are so many strangers passing through, to lose that element of privacy."

She felt Gage's shrug. "It's a way of life. It's not as if it was a closed place and then suddenly there was a wild influx of tourists."

"That's true. I guess it just comes from growing up on a farm. Lots of privacy there."

"Hmm. Boarding school and sharing a room with three other lads offered no privacy."

She turned her head and pressed a kiss to the column of his neck. "Did you have a lot of friends?"

"No. I was a surly bugger." His fingers played idly at her shoulder. "So, I take it you're not ready to pack up and move to Venice?"

She knew he was teasing, but still it struck a chord deep within her. "It's a uniquely beautiful place and I'm more than a little in love with it—the architecture, the food, the fact that I can walk anywhere. But do I love it enough to move here? No. I'm pretty sure the infatuation wouldn't stand up to the daily business of life. It's expensive, and while I like visiting a pedestrian city, I'm not sure I'd like living in one if I had to pick up groceries regularly, or take Ming to the vet. And then, of course, I'd miss little things like my language, my family, my career. But the thing that seals the deal? Julia is here. It's my intent to never cross Julia's path again."

"Excellent points, all of those."

"What about you? It sounds as if you travel all over Europe. Are you ever tempted to move? Have you ever found a place you simply fell in love with?"

"I can vouch that I don't particularly love London. However, it's a great gallery location and a very convenient hub for the rest of Europe. Prague is lovely. I'd say I'm more infatuated with it than any other place I've visited. You should consider it for your next travel adventure."

"Maybe." She snuggled against his side, content. "Are you trying to line up another guide job before I've even seen all of Venice?"

"That could work out well, since I already know what you like. Save some other bloke the learning curve. And actually, I was thinking more along the lines of a date than a business arrangement."

"A date?" She was beginning to think he wasn't teasing.

"Perhaps in the early fall, when the summer tourists have all flocked home."

A date? She'd known there was a chasm separating her world and Gage's, but the reality of it suddenly hit her. To her, a date was dinner and a movie. If it was really special, she and her escort might go to a musical or a play at Atlanta's Fox Theatre. For him a trans-Atlantic trip and then halfway across Europe again was a date. As it stood now, she could leave in two days and have scorching memories of a holiday fling. But what happened if they kept in touch?

"I'll have to check my work schedule. I'm one of those tourists who has a career to consider."

"Fair enough. But think about it, I think you'd fall in love with Prague, too."

"I think you're probably right."

Sex with Gage was good, make that great...actually, make that spectacular. She knew it would be far too easy to fall in love with Gage Carswell. And she also knew that falling in love with him was a supremely bad idea. Look at her parents. Infatuation had struck Farmer Smith and his International Model with disastrous results.

Maybe she'd rent a travel video and watch it when she got home, but that was about it. She didn't see a trip to Prague in her future. She would not repeat her parents' mistake.

12

"WE NEED YOU IN BUDAPEST," Mason said, his tone cold and clipped when he contacted Gage the next afternoon. "Tomorrow morning. You'll take the train from Venice tonight."

"Tonight? I've got another twelve hours on this assignment."

"I'm reassigning you. We'll bring in a replacement to finish up. Actually, a tail should be adequate at this juncture." Mason continued as if Gage hadn't spoken. "You depart Venice at 7:30 p.m. and arrive in Budapest at 9:30 a.m. We've had another Gorgon sighting. She'll arrive shortly after your train tomorrow, traveling as Sandy Walters." He then proceeded to fill Gage in on the rest of the details. Gage didn't recognize the hotel Mason mentioned, but he did recognize the street address. It was one of the seedier areas of Budapest where people tended to look the other way and not ask questions.

He concentrated on the particulars and ignored what felt like a gaping hole inside him. He'd known this was coming, just not so soon. "Same operational procedures?"

"Yes. Monitor her twenty-four/seven and report daily."

"Was Venice a decoy? A setup?" Budapest actually made more sense as a delivery point. The Gorgon's buyers, most likely from the Far or Middle East, would find it much easier to move in and out of Budapest than Venice.

"It's looking that way. We're not the only ones who maintain a list of look-alikes." Average citizens whose names and identities could be "borrowed" as a cover on occasion wasn't employed often but it was available. "Have you noticed any other agent activity?"

"None," he said.

"Bloody double-crossing Yanks. They lead us on a merry chase to Venice, and they keep what they know to themselves. Bloody bastards."

"Makes sense," Gage said, leaving it at that. It did make sense. That's why he hadn't uncovered any CIA agents on his tail. It explained a lot. But it struck Gage as being too pat, too slick. Or maybe it was just Mason's delivery that felt a bit too ready. There was a note of the rehearsed about it.

"We will, however, continue to monitor Ms. Smith until she departs Europe. Don't forget you need to arrive at the station half an hour before departure."

He hung up abruptly. Prick. Hadn't Gage managed to travel without Mason's input as to when he should arrive at the bloody train depot? Not that he'd been best blokes with the other handler he'd worked with for seven years, but dealing with Mason always left a faintly bitter taste in his mouth.

Mason's assertion when he'd first handed out this assignment, *if it walks like a Gorgon, talks like a Gorgon, it must be a Gorgon,* echoed in his head.

Gage had training in spades, but one thing an agent couldn't learn was instinct. And Gage's gut was screaming at him that something was wrong. This wasn't the first time he'd been pulled and reassigned at the end. Occasionally someone else was sent in for the clean-up, especially if Gage's surveillance skills were required elsewhere.

Setting a tail on Holly, having someone follow her from a distance, should be more than adequate. There was no rational reason he should feel compelled to stay with her, to protect her and watch over her until she was safely home. She should be free and clear of all danger, particularly with the Gorgon on the move to Budapest. He tried to shake off the feeling of dread hanging over him like a dark cloud.

He made quick work of packing his case and scrubbed a hand through his hair. Was it his gut truly sending him a warning or was it that somehow, somewhere along the line, Holly Smith had started to matter to him? Because the bloody bottom line was that he didn't want to leave her any sooner than he had to. He didn't want to hand her over to another operative. Was that skewing his judgment? But he'd been ordered to go, which left him no option. A rogue agent was ultimately a dead agent.

Bailing on her now was going to be sodding lovely. If he'd ever thought about her in terms beyond this assignment, and God help him, but the stray thought had crept in like a starving mongrel showing up at a door to steal scraps, this wouldn't improve his chances.

He locked the washroom door, retrieved the audio/video plant, and packed it with his other equipment. He didn't believe he'd have the opportunity to retrieve the bug in her room, but the washroom one could come in handy.

He knocked on the washroom door leading to her

room. Hers opened and she stood there, resplendent with the silk robe knotted loosely at her waist and her hair pulled up and back, the same as she'd worn it last night. Her loveliness took his breath.

"Was there something I could help you with before dinner, Mr. Carswell?" Her flirtatious drawl and the coy invitation in her eyes left no doubt exactly what kind of help was available. Her nipples pebbled against the silk. Christ, she was naked beneath the robe.

He shouldn't, he really shouldn't, but he couldn't seem to stop himself from reaching for her. She came willingly, wrapping her arms around his waist. Soft, warm, silk robe and satin skin.

He stood there, simply holding her for a long moment, wanting to take the feel of her with him.

"What's wrong, Gage?" she asked. "Something's upset you."

And he felt her confusion. It wasn't just the questioning look in her eyes, he *felt* it. He cradled her jaw in his hand, smoothing his thumb over the ridge of her cheekbone.

Then he abruptly dropped his hand and stepped away. If he didn't quit touching her, he'd never get done what needed to be done. "Something unexpected's come up and I have to leave tonight."

Confusion and no small measure of hurt clouded her eyes. "But I had you contracted through tomorrow."

"The agency will refund your entire fee." Mason could squeeze the pounds out of his expense budget. "It's the least we can do for all the abrupt changes in your schedule."

She drew herself even more upright. "That's not necessary."

"I'm sure they'll insist."

Her smile held that same brittle edge it had when they'd left her mother's house. "What exotic location are you off to now?"

"Paris." Even if he was one-hundred-percent certain she wasn't the Gorgon, he still couldn't tell her his true destination.

She didn't challenge him, but her look said she knew he was lying. "Another tour-guide position? The gallery? Personal business?"

"Gallery business and it's rather pressing. I have to leave tonight."

She wrapped her arms around her middle. "I see." The only thing she saw was that he was leaving early and lying about his reasons.

He nearly asked if he could call her when he got back, but how fair was that to her? What kind of relationship could they have? He was lying to her and she knew it. He was very adept at deception, but whatever this thing was between them, she seemed to see to his core.

And while he'd had to lie about his destination, the rest, well, he'd stick with the truth. "The past four days have been some of the best days of my life, Holly. Thank you." All good things must come to an end.

"It was pretty wonderful, wasn't it?" She laughed again, not able to hide that edge to her voice. He knew she was hurting inside and he hated himself for being the one in-flicting the pain. "But then again, it's a pretty wonderful city."

It wasn't just the city. It was them—the two of them together. She knew it. He knew it. But he'd give her an out.

What the hell was wrong with him? He knew how to conduct an exit. Clean, swift, simple. Not standing about dithering like a callow school lad.

"Right, then. Have a safe trip home."

"Have a safe trip to Paris."

He turned for the door and then swung around again, reaching into his pocket for his business card case. He pulled out one of the black, high-gloss cards with the gallery name and address and placed it on the desk. "This is my gallery in London. If you're ever in town, give us a lookup." And he knew he shouldn't continue, but he couldn't seem to stop himself, "And if you ever need anything, luv, you can reach me there. Or, at least, Agnes will be able to find me."

She left the card where it lay on the table. "Sure." She offered a perfunctory nod. "I'll keep that in mind if I'm ever in London."

He wanted to touch her just one last time. He reached for her and she stepped back, shaking her head. "Just go."

He went.

HOLLY HEARD THE DOOR to the hallway close and the measured tread of Gage's footsteps gradually fade as he walked down the hall.

It was done. Over with. It seemed foolish for her to feel so hollow and empty inside, yet she did. So she'd missed out on one more night and possibly an early morning of mind-altering sex. It was disappointing, but hardly devastating. It wasn't the first night she'd spent alone nor would it be the last.

Maybe she should go out and find an Italian lover for her last night in Venice…. No, she couldn't. It wasn't like her. And worse yet, that lover wouldn't be Gage. Since Gage was the man she wanted, it was best to just leave well enough alone. She'd known from the beginning, from the first time she saw him, that they were from different worlds. It had been a holiday fling, destined from the beginning to end within the week. It couldn't be anything more. Her recent family history proved that.

She crossed to the window and opened the shutter, but even the charm of the curving stone street and Old World architecture failed to lighten her mood. Gage emerged from the pensione's front door to the street below, broad shoulders, dark hair, erect carriage, his travel bag and laptop case slung over one shoulder. A woman walking in the opposite direction noticed him, turning, in fact, after she'd passed to continue looking.

Women would always notice Gage Carswell. Holly watched him stride down the street, obviously a man in a hurry. She didn't know where he was going, but it definitely wasn't Paris. She also didn't know why he couldn't have just told her the truth. She was a big girl. But he hadn't, so that was that.

He paused at the curve in the street, which would take him out of sight, turned and looked up. Even from this distance, his dark eyes captured and held hers.

He turned and walked on, swallowed by the road's curve. End of her holiday romance. End of story.

Why, then, did it feel as if he'd taken a part of her with him?

From the nightstand her cell phone rang. She ran across the room and snatched it up. Maybe he'd changed his mind…. She glanced at caller ID and groaned, seeing her cousin's name on the display. She wasn't up to talking to

Josephine. She wasn't up to talking to anyone. If she were at home she'd let it go to voice mail, but she wasn't at home. What if an emergency had cropped up?

She answered the call.

GAGE SETTLED BACK AGAINST the functional train carriage upholstery. Nothing was going according to plan. The night train, usually very efficient, was experiencing a mechanical delay. He closed his eyes and once again saw Holly framed in the window of the Pensione Armand. His mobile phone vibrated against his side.

He answered. The desk clerk from the Pensione Armand spoke rapidly and he repeated it back to make sure he'd heard her correctly.

"Si, si."

He'd been gone little more than an hour and a package had turned up for Signora Smith. Sometimes life was full of coincidences, but not usually. This situation struck him as being anything but.

He thanked the woman for letting him know and asked her to hold the package, telling her he'd like to surprise Signora Smith with it himself. Luckily for him, the clerk was a romantic. He could practically hear her sigh as he hung up the phone. Equally lucky for him, he'd left without officially checking out. The room had been let through until tomorrow, so he hadn't seen the point. As an operative, he seldom announced his leaving, especially when he left ahead of schedule.

He'd better alert Mason. He hesitated, his finger on the speed dial number programmed for his handler. Gage's internal alarms clanged. Mason had been adamant Gage leave tonight. Mason had also sent him in on this job without immunity, not an uncommon status, but a bit extreme for a watch-and-see assignment. Mason's claim that the Americans had double-crossed them had come across a tad too…something. It simply hadn't felt right.

A voice came over the train PA, announcing they'd be departing the station in two minutes.

Every instinct Gage possessed clamored for him to get off the train and go back to Holly, that whatever was in the package that had been delivered *after* his departure meant danger for her.

Gage made a split decision. He shoved his phone into his case and his case into the compartment bin of the train. His mobile came GPS-enabled. Even if he couldn't be contacted, he could be tracked. Quite suddenly Gage wasn't so fond of having his movements known. It struck him that letting Mason believe he'd left Venice was exactly the thing to do. If his handler had been straight up with him, then Gage would manufacture a lie to cover himself. If Mason hadn't, then far better that he not be privy to his exact location. He slung his laptop case over his shoulder and made his move.

Stepping out into the train's central aisle, he closed the compartment door behind him and nonchalantly made his way toward the washroom at the end of the car. He knew from the assessment he'd taken when he arrived that cameras scanned the platform adjacent to the station, to the left of the car but not to the right.

His hands thrust casually into his trouser pockets, Gage stepped off the train onto the right-hand platform. He paused next to a column until the camera near the stairs scanned to the far left. Then he crossed the platform to the stairs.

Another couple of camera maneuvers and he'd cleared the Stazione Santa Lucia and exited to the broad terrace along the Grand Canal with the vaporetto and water taxi landings.

He queued for a spot on the vaporetto. The water taxi would be quicker, but he'd stand out less in a crowd.

An hour later he stopped at Pensione Armand's front desk, having stopped along the way to purchase a pay-as-you-go mobile phone.

"A package arrived for Ms. Smith?" he asked in Italian.

"Si." She indicated a large cardboard box behind her, the airline label clearly visible. He was willing to wager, well, his life, that Holly Smith's missing luggage had miraculously shown up. As a rule, operatives were extremely leery of miracles.

"Grazie."

He hauled the oversize cardboard box with him upstairs, pausing on the landing between the second and third floor. He reached into his pocket and fingered the listening device that he'd pocketed rather than packed. He flipped the switch. Not only did it detect audio bugs he'd set, it had the capability of picking up other audio feed. If a bug had been planted in her case, he'd feel a vibration as it picked up the frequency.

No bug.

He continued until he stood outside Holly's room. He knocked quietly.

Her voice was muffled from the other side. "Yes?"

"It's Gage, Holly. I need to talk to you."

He wasn't altogether sure she'd open the door. She did, but she didn't appear prepared to invite him in.

"What about Paris?"

"I'd rather discuss this inside, if you don't mind."

He saw it in her face the moment she made her decision. She moved aside. "Come in."

He stepped into the room, hauling the box in with him, and closed the door. Relief at finding her safe and sound flooded him. He pushed her against the wall and ground his mouth, his body against hers, desperate to touch her, taste her again.

Holly pushed him away and straightened from the wall, her expression clearly telling him they weren't just taking up where they left off.

She nodded toward the box sitting just inside the door. "This is for me?"

"Yes."

A puzzled frown appeared on her face. She looked at the return label on the box. "What the heck?" Holly grabbed a tear strip and pulled, causing the cardboard to give way.

"I don't believe this. Then again with the way the rest of this trip has gone, sure, I believe it!" She burst out laughing.

"What's so funny?" Gage asked.

"The timing is priceless. I go home tomorrow—" she pulled down one side of the cardboard to reveal a black nylon-canvas case "—and my suitcase is delivered today."

"Are you sure that's your suitcase? Maybe it's a replacement."

"No. It had this scuff mark on it." She dragged it out and unzipped the top. "Yep. It looks as if everything's here. They're all rolled just the way I packed them."

He watched her carefully. He'd spent four days and nights observing her even when she thought herself unobserved. He'd know if she was lying. "Well, that's a surprise, isn't it?"

"Definitely. I'd given up on it after the first day. Now it arrives just in time for me to drag it back home. It's crazy."

"Definitely crazy."

We destroyed it, ripped out the seams in her trousers and knickers, even took the case locks apart. Nothing.

Mason had lied. The case hadn't even been touched. And it had conveniently not shown up until he was supposedly en route to Budapest.

What else had his handler lied about?

13

THE GORGON HUMMED TO herself as she changed clothes, readying herself for her final rendezvous with Brad and Tim. By this time tomorrow, she'd be long gone. Better yet, by this time tomorrow, Holly would be permanently gone, taken out by a sniper's bullet after she delivered the package. The Eastern European assassin the Gorgon had hired didn't miss. Holly was as good as dead.

The Gorgon danced around her bedroom in celebration.

She really hadn't realized just how much she hated the annoying bitch until the opportunity to kill her had presented itself. Actually, the Gorgon considered it fate's gift when Holly announced her intention to find her mother in Venice—an opportunity for Holly to atone for the misery she'd heaped on the Gorgon.

The Gorgon had always adored her uncle Charles. And when the Gorgon's parents had been killed, she'd wanted to live with him. But he already had his precious Holly. So, instead, she had been packed off to her grandmother's. Everyone had expected her and Holly to be as close as sisters, since they were both motherless little girls and they looked so much alike. The very thought that Holly had *her* eyes made her want to scratch them out of Holly's head. Except she'd gone one better.

It'd been like leading a stupid sheep to slaughter. She'd set up a fictitious travel guide company on the Internet and then recommended it to Holly. It had been ridiculously easy and the little incompetent had fallen for it. The Gorgon laughed. Holly had even paid her for it. Beautiful.

They'd covered all the bases. Carswell had been dispatched to Budapest where another assassin's bullet awaited him.

Holly Smith would be tagged as the dead Gorgon and the world would be short one British operative. Boo hoo.

There was one wrinkle, however, one she hadn't been able to work out. She crossed to the goldfish bowl where Fishy trustingly swam about. She couldn't take Fishy with her. It would be impossible to clear Customs with a goldfish. And if she left him here on his own, he'd starve to death. The thought was unbearable.

She knew what she had to do but it was so hard. She drew a deep fortifying breath and scooped Fishy out of the tank with the net. She couldn't look at him flopping desperately in the mesh as she hurried down the hall. She heard the plop as he hit the water in the toilet bowl, but she still couldn't look when she flushed.

Tears flowed in a swift salty river down her cheeks. Sometimes life just sucked.

GAGE WAS ONE MISSING puzzle piece away.

"Holly, I have a question for you. It's rather important."

She crossed her arms over her chest, a stubborn light in her eyes. "You left, saying you were going to Paris, and now you show up again a few hours later. And you have questions for me? I think you've got to come up with a few answers of your own first."

"I promise I'll tell you why I lied about Paris—"

"So you did lie."

"I did. And I promise I'll give you an answer, but I need to know this first."

"Okay," she finally said.

"Are you aware of anyone you look like? Anyone someone might mistake you for? Specifically anyone with your unusual eye color?"

Despite her wary expression, she nodded slowly. "My cousin, Josephine. She's two years older than I am, but the family resemblance is very strong."

"She's your cousin?"

Holly nodded, still perplexed. "People have always said we could be sisters. And it's always irritated her that I have *her* eye color. I could tell she was thrilled when I started wearing colored contact lenses and was really upset when I stopped." Bloody bingo. "She's one of those people that only bothers to be nice when she wants something." She seemed to be chatting almost nervously. "Like when she found out I was coming to Venice, she suggested your tour guide company."

"She travels a good bit?"

"Something with her job. So it seems as if she's done me a favor, recommending a tour-guide service. But right before I left, she asked me to look up a friend of hers and deliver a present. I was off the hook until my suitcase showed back up."

"The present is in your case?"

She laughed awkwardly and shrugged. "Yep. Now I have a delivery to make. After all, she's family. Why? And why are you looking so grim?"

He quickly weighed his options. There was only one. He

had to get the package and get her out of this situation. None of that was going to happen without revealing his identity.

"I'm going to try to make this brief. I'm sure you'll have questions, but time is of the essence and you're going to have to trust me. My name *is* Gage Carswell, I *do* own an art gallery in London, but I'm *not* a tour guide. I'm an undercover British operative. Are you with me so far?"

"Are you saying you're a spy?"

"Right in one."

"I think I'm going to be sick." She made a mad dash for the washroom.

WELL, THERE WAS NOTHING quite like puking to set the mood, Holly thought as she brushed her teeth and rinsed with mouthwash.

She opened the bathroom door to find Gage, at least he said that was his real name, waiting in her room. "Are you okay?"

He looked concerned, but honestly she was so confused she didn't know what was and wasn't real anymore. "I'm fine. Just surprised."

His curt nod stiffened her backbone. "Tell me about this present you're supposed to deliver for your cousin."

"When she heard I was coming to Venice she said a friend of hers from college lived here. The woman had recently married and Josephine wanted me to drop off a wedding gift for her. She said it was less likely to get broken if I brought it with me." She opened her suitcase and pulled out a small gift-wrapped package.

"Did she tell you what it was?"

"A picture frame. I was just glad it was small and wouldn't take up too much room in my suitcase." Holly couldn't ignore the hard edge of his smile. "I was an idiot, wasn't I?"

"How could you know? You don't find an international spy at your family dinner table on a regular basis." A woman also didn't find she'd been sleeping with an international spy every day, either. "I think you can excuse yourself for not knowing." He held out his hand for the package. "May I?"

It was rhetorical, because he could obviously take it from her if she said no. Still, she found it oddly gallant he asked. She handed over the package.

He opened it, taking care not to rip either the tape or the paper. He lifted the box lid, revealing a rather ornate five-by-seven silver picture frame with black velvet backing. He lifted the back, pulled a small instrument from his pocket and pried at an almost invisible seam on the silver.

The front popped apart from the back, revealing a hollow channel. Two small disks, larger than a dime but smaller than a quarter, encapsulated in plastic were affixed in the channel. Gage gently pried them out.

Holly's mind literally whirled. "Oh, my God." She sank to the edge of the bed, trying to assimilate everything. She clenched her hands into fists to try to control them from shaking. "What's this all about? Explain it to me. Just start from the beginning."

She listened without comment to the background he'd received on Josephine, whom he referred to as the Gorgon. He then went on to explain how Holly had been mistaken as the Gorgon in London, and Gage's assignment to the job. She stopped him.

"You mean that your boss was responsible for my plane sitting on the runway all those hours? He arranged that?"

He nodded brusquely. "I needed time to arrive and set up—"

"Set up?"

"An audio/video feed."

"You bugged my room?" She hated that her voice shook on that last note.

"Yes. It was my job. You were my assignment from the time you arrived at the Venice airport."

"You were at the airport? I never saw you."

A hard smile accompanied his nod. "And on the vaporetto. You didn't see me then, either, because I didn't want you to."

"You're good at what you do?"

He shrugged. "I'm still alive."

"And was it part of your assignment to sleep with me?"

"If necessary. But it wasn't. I'd already concluded at that point that you weren't the Gorgon."

"And when did you know I wasn't this Gorgon?" She was proud that her voice didn't even quiver.

"When you got back from that meeting with your mother."

Before he'd come to her and they'd made love for the first time. There was a small measure of comfort in that, at least.

She said nothing and he continued on with his tale, about his reassignment to Budapest and the subsequent phone call from the Pensione Armand. He knew everything there was to know about her. She felt—she didn't want to think about how she felt right now. She could at least keep that much of herself private.

"That was smart of you to send your luggage on the train with your phone."

He shrugged. "It just buys us a little time. If Mason had someone on the train watching for me, then he already knows I'm not on it. I suspect, however, that he's working minimally, which means he won't know for sure until the train arrives in Budapest tomorrow morning. So, back to this package. How, when and where were you to deliver it?"

"Her friend was returning from her honeymoon today. I was supposed to drop the package off to her tomorrow on my way to the airport."

"Where?"

She relayed the address. "When Jo gave me the street number, she said it was easy to remember because it was the same as my street address at home." None of this made sense to her. "What do you think it means? Why would they send you?"

"Mason and the Gorgon have to be working together. Mason's my handler. Given all of the circumstances, this is the way I think it's meant to play out." He cleared his throat and checked that Holly wasn't about to throw up again. "Normally a mule, or, in this case, you, is just a delivery vehicle. You'd make your drop and go on your way, none the wiser." He hesitated and she caught a flash of concern.

"What? Tell me."

He squared his shoulders and spoke crisply, looking past her rather than at her. "That's under normal circumstance. I don't believe, however, that there's anything normal about this situation. We've been closing in on the Gorgon, and the CIA is probably doing the same. It's far more likely, in my opinion, that you're to be terminated after the drop. Then the Gorgon is taken care of and no one need look for her any longer."

"Terminated. You mean…"

"Rather euphemistic, isn't it? Yes. Killed." He still didn't look at her. She realized that in his own way, he was affording her a small measure of privacy to deal with the reality that in all probability, a member of her family had arranged her murder.

She swallowed. Terminated. Killed. It just sort of bounced off of her. No doubt it would hit her later. "Oh. And you?"

"I think I was sent to verify that Mason was doing his job. I'm certain I was to be terminated, as well, in Budapest."

Her heart threatened to beat out of her chest. She'd probably been in a mild state of shock before, which was rather insulating. Now the situation was becoming terrifyingly real. She gasped.

He looked at her and she found the competency and calm in his dark eyes bracing. "Holly, I know you're frightened. I also know you're terribly practical. Do you happen to have a pair of scissors and a sewing kit in your toiletry?"

She nodded.

"Excellent. That's my girl. Bring me the scissors, your robe and nightgown and one of those black blouses."

"You're going to cut my clothes?"

"Once it gets a bit darker outside, we've got to change locations. In the meantime, we're going to tart you up. They'll be looking for a rather ordinary woman with extraordinary eyes. We need to transform you into something else."

An ordinary woman with extraordinary eyes. She knew it, but it felt like a slap in the face to hear the words coming from him. She stood silently by as he efficiently cut her gown and robe and sewed in a hem, transforming them to a silk camisole top and a matching jacket. Next he cut out and hemmed a large black square from her blouse. He spread the lower-half-robe remnant on the floor. "Sit here. I'll cut your hair. We'll wrap it up in the material and take it with us. If they search here, they won't find anything to tip them off your hair's been altered."

She was too numb to argue. He stopped her as she started to sit. "Take off your trousers and blouse. You don't want hair all over them."

She stripped down to her underwear and sat on the edge of the fabric. It was almost like sitting half naked in front of a stranger. She wasn't sure if the man she'd taken as a lover truly existed.

The unyielding floor pressed hard and chilly against the back of her thighs. He ran his fingers through her hair and held a piece aloft. He might be a stranger, but his touch was the same. Even in the midst of everything falling apart around her, a tremor coursed through her as his knuckles grazed her scalp and his scent enveloped her like a blanket of comforting familiarity. Except for the snip of the scissors, quiet permeated the room. Cool air settled against her neck where he cut the length away.

She worried her lower lip between her teeth. She would not, could not, sit around and allow this to unfold around her while she waited to see what happened next. She had to take a proactive stance. That meant understanding all aspects of what was going on around her. "What's going to happen to Josephine?"

"There are three possible scenarios. The least likely is she'll manage to escape and live on the run. It's also not probable, but possible, she'll be terminated. The most likely, though, is she'll be arrested and prosecuted."

Holly stiffened her spine. "How can I help?"

"I'll need her full name, phone number, address. Everything you can tell me about her."

Holly reminded herself she wasn't betraying her cousin. After all, Josephine had set her up, trying to use her to deliver international secrets. By rights, they should've been close. There wasn't much of an age difference, they'd looked similar, and both girls had grown up in a less-than-ideal family. But there'd never been a real connection. Yet Holly could hardly fathom how someone she knew got to the point that she'd betray everyone and everything, her own country, for money.

Gage interrupted her thoughts. "I don't suppose you actually have colored contacts, do you?"

"No." She'd made a statement to herself by tossing the remaining pairs months ago.

"Didn't think so. It would've made things too easy. Those magnificent eyes of yours are your identifying mark."

He snipped and stepped back to assess her. He nodded. "That'll do. Take off your bra and put on the nightgown top and robe. Go heavier on the makeup than usual."

"I'm going to look like a hooker."

"That's the idea. We're going to a hotel that rents rooms by the hour. No one will ask questions and no one will care that we show up near midnight without luggage. So set your practical mind to looking like a tart, luv."

She laughed, and for a second, she felt as if she might slip over the edge to hysteria. "Okay."

He folded the fabric on the floor into a neat square, and with a few quick stitches, sewed it up. "Leave everything except your makeup, toothbrush and two sets of knickers. Bring along the sewing kit and scissors. Also pack a torch if you have one." He handed her the fabric. "Put this in the bottom of your knapsack and we'll dispose of it later."

She took the fabric and put it in her bag. "I have a small travel flashlight."

"Splendid. Once you've done your hair and makeup, slip the other black blouse over your top and put this on as a scarf." He handed her the black square of fabric he'd hemmed. "Put those sexy sandals in your knapsack. Wear the black flats. If anyone sees us leaving, they need to see you dressed as you usually are."

"The rather ordinary woman."

"Precisely. We leave in ten minutes."

"Then I'd better get busy."

He stilled her with a hand to her arm. "Holly, I think we have the element of surprise on our side, but if things go wrong, if anything should happen to me, tell them whatever they want to know. Immediately. Don't try to be heroic."

"But if I tell them what they want to know, won't that compromise other people? Do you think it will stop them from killing me?"

There was a grimness around his mouth and a flash of pity for her naiveté in his eyes that truly frightened her. "Luv, if they catch you, they'll kill you regardless. It will simply be far less unpleasant if you talk first."

14

"EXCELLENT," GAGE SAID as Holly appeared by the door with one minute to spare. She really was quite an amazing woman. There'd been a refreshing lack of histrionics on her part as he revealed their situation. She'd tied the scarf beneath her chin and with the black-on-black outfit and the additional makeup darkening her eyes, she looked exactly as he'd anticipated. "Very sophisticated. Very European. Don't speak, though. That will give away the fact that you're an American. If someone approaches us, act as if you don't know what they're saying. I'll speak to you in Latvian."

"But I don't understand Latvian."

"That's fine. Just look as if you do."

Gage debated whether to discuss the contingency plan with her. He didn't want to rattle her, yet he wanted her to have the best chance for survival if something happened to him. She was strong. She could manage. "One always hopes for the best but prepares for the worst. In the event that I don't come out of this alive, you're to go as quickly as possible to 371 Calle Lungo on the island of Burano. Take the vaporetto."

She interrupted him. "Wait. Let me write it down."

"No. Memorize it. If it's written down, someone else

could find it and read it. Ask for Giuseppe. He's a fisherman. Tell him I sent you and tell him you need to get to Rome without going by train or plane."

"Rome?"

"Rome. He'll secure you a lorry ride. Go directly to the U.S. Embassy there. Tell them everything. Do not contact your father or any family members. And for God's sake, whatever you do, don't part with that package. It's your life insurance policy. How much cash do you have?"

"Two hundred American dollars in traveler's checks and a little over one hundred euros."

"That's enough to get home, but not enough if you're sidetracked. Here are four hundred more euros. Take them."

She took the money and put it in the small belt she wore inside her trousers, along with her passport.

"Now, to the left of your room, just outside the door, is another door at the end of the hall. It rather looks as if it might be a closet, but it leads to a staircase that's a servants' stairway. We're going down to the basement and we'll come out canal side. I'll need your torch."

He glimpsed her first hint of panic as she pulled the torch out of her knapsack. "We don't have to swim in the canal, do we?"

"No. We're going to *borrow* the skiff moored there."

"Thank God," she muttered.

"Once we're a couple of canals over, we'll leave the skiff and take a vaporreto to Mestre, which is close to the airport. Ready?"

She smiled grimly. "Let's do this thing."

Gage clasped her hand in his, listened at the door and then opened it. They stepped out into the hall. Muffled voices sounded from behind a closed door farther down, but no one was out and about. He opened the servants' quarter door he'd discovered his first night here and pulled her into the stairwell behind him, easing the door closed behind them.

He stood for a moment, letting their eyes adjust to the dark, and he squeezed her hand for reassurance. She squeezed back and he found himself grinning like a sodding nutter. He leaned in close until his mouth grazed her ear. "Slow and quiet."

He felt her nod against his face. He flipped on the switch of the torch, directing the light at the stairs. They set off, feeling their way with one hand against the plaster wall. No handrail on these stairs, he supposed, because the servants' hands were always full carrying something.

They were just outside the basement, which had no door separating it from the stairwell, when something scuttled over their feet, most likely a mouse. While Holly started, she didn't as much as squeak. Gage quickly tugged her across the room. In less than a minute they were in the small skiff. Gage rowed away from the dock and down the canal. He couldn't risk starting the small outboard motor just yet.

The canal curved to the right and Holly whispered from the seat in front of him. "If you're through with my flashlight, I'll put it away."

He returned her torch, his fingers brushing hers in the exchange, making sure she had a good grip before he re-linquished it.

"What's the plan? I'm sure you have one," she said. "I'd rather not sit idly by wondering how we're going to get out of this."

It was rather flattering that she seemed totally confident he would, indeed, get them out of this double-crossed stew. And yes, he did have a plan.

"At this juncture I'm not sure who might be in this above Mason on my side, so the first thing I'm going to do is contact your government's CIA. They're as bloody rabid to stop the Gorgon as we are. Then, tomorrow morning, I'll ring Mason and get a bleed on his line."

"A bleed?"

"Right. I'll be privy to all of his incoming and outgoing calls. Rather like a three-way call, but he can't hear me on my end."

"Isn't that illegal?"

"I rather suspect it might be, but you shouldn't worry about that. I'm fairly certain, with some well-placed lies on my part fanning his paranoia and misogynistic inclination, he'll proceed to hang himself."

"And if he doesn't?"

"Then I get you to the embassy in Rome and Mason and I will engage in a game of hide-and-seek."

"But what if he finds you?"

"I won't be the one hiding, luv."

He didn't miss her shiver. "I can't say I like it, but at least I understand how it would benefit Josephine for everyone to think she was dead. But why would Mason order you killed? And why would he send you to Budapest to have it done? It doesn't make sense."

Gage had thought the same thing. He'd worked it from every angle, and quite simply it made no sense that Mason would have him terminated in conjunction with Holly and the Gorgon. Which left him looking outside of what made sense. "I've got a theory that my termination has nothing to do with you. Still, throwing it in there confuses the issue and leaves one looking for the logical link that doesn't exist."

He quickly explained the role of a stringer in their business, and how money was allocated to stringers based on the merit of the information they brought in. He explained how in his job, he often found valuable information that wasn't necessarily what he'd been assigned to uncover. "Last month I discovered contact information on illegal organs, harvesters, buyers. It's a lucrative business that preys on the poor and ill-informed. That information would've earned a stringer top money."

"And let me guess, Mason allocates money to his stringers."

"Got it in one."

"And if he was working with Josephine, then he wouldn't be above creating an allocation for a stringer who doesn't exist and pocketing the money." He nodded. "But he needed to get rid of you, in case the information ever came up again."

"Precisely."

"And there's no reason why he should send you to Budapest when you could be terminated in Venice. So that's exactly why he sent you, to muddy the waters."

"Bloody brilliant you are, luv," he said, pulling up to a public docking station.

"He won't stop until you're dead, will he?"

"I prefer to look at it as I simply have to trap him first." He tied up the boat to the pole and helped her out onto the quay.

Gage would've liked to attribute the surge in his pulse to having completed that first step, but a bloke needed to

at least be honest with himself. It had everything to do
with the woman. Holly with her quixotic mix of practi-
cality, sensuality and passion was responsible for the
rapid-fire rate of his heart.

He hoped like bloody hell he didn't wind up getting
her killed.

"WELL, THIS DEFINITELY wasn't on my must-see list,"
Holly said, mustering a smile. "But you were absolutely
right. The clerk barely blinked an eye when we asked for
a room for the night."

"He was probably surprised, though. Most of the
business here is concluded in a much shorter time frame."

The Mestre, an industrialized area on the mainland,
faced Venice across the lagoon. They'd traded Old World
elegance for postmodern industrialization complete with
street traffic, rows of factories and oil refineries belching
black smoke into the night.

Their small, dingy hotel room made no pretense of ac-
commodating long-term occupation. There was no dresser
or wardrobe. The furniture consisted of a bed, a nightstand, a chair and a very large mirror facing the bed.
Cracked and peeling plaster and a bedside lamp without
a shade completed the ambience. The coin-operated
condom dispenser located on the wall lent an elegant
touch. Holly suppressed a shudder.

"Are you worried about germs?"

Obviously she hadn't done such a good job of sup-
pressing anything. "Oddly enough, no. It's just such a sad
place. How many women spend an hour here with a loathsome stranger because they don't have a choice, only to
find themselves with another stranger a few hours later?"

"It's a very old profession, Holly."

"I know. Old Venice was known for their courtesans. But it was considered elegant and almost respectable back then. But here? There's a shabbiness and sadness about this place."

As if to punctuate her remark, a rhythmic banging of a headboard resounded on the other side of the wall.

"It's late, you should get some rest."

She hadn't bargained for any of this. And yes, in a crazy way, she wouldn't trade a second of it. The hotel accommodated couples having sex as a matter of business.

How many of those women were lucky enough to lie in this bed with a man they loved? She'd known her true feelings when he left earlier tonight, but she hadn't been prepared to face them. Or maybe she'd known at the end of that gondola ride? What did the timing matter, anyway? Somewhere along the way, she'd fallen in love with Gage Carswell. She'd thought when he revealed his true identity, she'd think of him as a stranger. Not true. It was merely another facet of the man she'd fallen for.

Who knew what tomorrow might bring? One or both of them could be dead. Or she might be on her way back to Atlanta. He'd initiated contact with the CIA, and she was cautiously optimistic Gage's plan would work. Regardless, she wasn't wasting a second of this night on sleep.

She was a little unsure of herself. He hadn't touched her in even a remotely sensual way since he'd revealed his true identity. He'd told her she was an ordinary woman. She'd never know for sure that he hadn't slept with her because he thought there was information to be had. All of that whispered through her head, but she shoved it all aside because in the end it simply didn't matter. Once upon a time, she would've waited for him to make a move, set the tone. Not now. Never again.

"I'm not sleepy." She untied the sash at her waist of the robe that had become a silk jacket. She slid it off of one shoulder and his eyes darkened. She rolled her shoulders, letting it slide off of the other shoulder.

She didn't look away from him as she unbuttoned and unzipped her pants. She swallowed hard and shelved her germ concerns and let the pants drop to the floor. She stepped clear of the garment puddled on the floor, ever thankful that her heels didn't get caught in the material.

She stood in front of him clad in her high-heeled strappy sandals she'd changed back into after leaving the Pensione, black panties and a silk top that plunged to her waist and bared her soul.

"Make love to me. Not because you need information, not because it might blow your cover if you don't. Make love to me because you want to."

SHE SHOULD BE TERRIFIED and worried sick about tomorrow. Instead, she was oddly calm. There was a sense of contentment about lying naked in Gage's arms. Tomorrow would bring whatever it would. If these were her last few hours, she wouldn't squander them on worry, or sleep.

She rolled to her side and settled her head on his shoulder. The sheets were rougher and coarser than at the Pensione Armand, but they smelled of the sun and the tinge of sea particular to Venice.

"How did you decide to become an agent?" she asked, breathing in his scent in the dark.

He ran his fingers through her hair. "I like your hair short like that. It's very becoming, very sexy," he said.

"So you said earlier." If he chose to ignore her question, that was fine. She certainly wasn't going to press the issue. Ultimately it didn't particularly matter, except she wanted to fill in the smaller gaps of who and what he was.

"I was recruited out of university. I was the perfect candidate. No close personal ties. Very little family, nobody I was close to."

"How old were you?"

"Twenty-two. I've been in the business for ten years."

"We don't have to talk about it if you don't want to."

"I don't mind. I simply don't know how to talk about it."

"Does anyone know?"

"Perhaps over the years, people have had some suspicions."

"So, you don't talk about it ever?"

"No. If too many people discovered who and what I am, then I'd be too vulnerable to be useful."

"And now that I know?"

"One way or another, this is my last assignment. Mason has already seen to that, and yes, now you know. I knew it when I got off of the train and came back. Mason will either kill me or I'll expose myself in exposing him."

He sounded so matter-of-fact about it. She supposed that was what he dealt with on each assignment. "Is it always kill or be killed?"

"No. My assignment wasn't to terminate you. I was simply to watch you twenty-four/seven, discover who and what you knew, intercept your contacts and your information and let you go."

"And if your orders had been to terminate me?"

"Then we wouldn't be having this conversation." She couldn't suppress a shudder. "Yet another reason it's best not to discuss my job. So tell me about teaching."

"We can change the topic without my boring you to tears telling you about my job."

"I asked because I want to know, Holly."

They lay for hours, talking about anything and everything. The dark invited confidences and the knowledge of what the next day could bring brought an honesty, a bluntness, a baring of souls....

Holly felt as if Gage Carswell knew her better than anyone ever had. And she instinctively knew he'd let her venture into private spaces with him where no one had gone before. They'd been lovers this week. Tonight they'd become friends.

FOR THE FIRST TIME since he'd gotten the shit kicked out of him that first day at boarding school, Gage was scared.

He'd lost people before during operations. Another operative. There'd been a civilian mishap once. Both had been very regretful. But the prospect of any harm coming to Holly gnawed in his gut like acid. It was as if he'd found a part of himself—the good part, the feeling part that had been closed off for so many years, in her.

"Holly..." He said her name softly, testing whether she was awake.

"Hmm?"

"I'm going to turn on the light."

"Why? It's nice in the dark."

He chuckled. "Can't see the squalid room? Sorry, luv. Cover your eyes." He snapped on the light. The room looked as dingy as ever.

"It's much more tolerable with the light out." She removed her hand. "This better be good."

Movement beyond her caught his eye. A cockroach scuttled across the wall, running away from the light. There'd be hell to pay if she saw that thing.

"I love you," he said without preamble, leaving the words to stand alone in their stark beauty.

Her gaze locked on to his, full of caution. "Don't say it if you don't mean it." She looked down and smoothed the sheet's edge with a finger. "That would be cruel. I think you're a hard man because you have to be, but you're not cruel."

He stilled her hand with his, wrapping her smaller one in his large palm. "I've never said that before to any woman. Those three words belong to you. They're yours. Do with them what you will."

"There's only one thing I can do." She looked up at him, turning her hand over beneath his, palm to palm, intertwining her fingers with his. "Echo them back to you. I love you."

Gage moved through life self-assured, confident of himself and his abilities. But he felt a sudden rush of debilitating insecurity that she could actually love him, embrace him, emotional scars and all. He withdrew his hand. "It's not a tit for tat. You don't have to say it back."

She laughed. The wretched woman actually laughed. "You stupid man." She pushed him onto his back. "I suppose I'll just have to show you."

15

"THEY WON'T HURT HER, will they?" Holly asked the next morning when Gage hung up after another conversation with the CIA. They'd confirmed the Gorgon's address and that she was home. As it stood now, they had her under constant surveillance.

"They shouldn't. It will actually work to her benefit if they surprise her. If she's running, she's more likely to get…hurt." He'd nearly said "terminated." Her cousin had set her up to be killed and yet Holly still worried about her. "If they, along with us, intercept a call to her from Mason, it will certainly help build a case."

"And you're recording your phone call to Mason?"

"Luv, I'm recording all of it."

"That's pretty amazing."

He grinned like a schoolboy. Christ, he felt like a lad showing off for the new girl, but it felt wanking good to have her look at him as if he were brilliant. "All in a day's work."

He rang Mason.

"Where the hell are you?"

"I had to wait until a kiosk opened to buy a mobile or I would've rung you earlier. I missed my train to Budapest."

"How'd you do that? And why didn't you have your mobile with you?"

"I thought I spotted the Gorgon and I dashed off the train. It got left behind."

"The Gorgon is now in Budapest. How could you have spotted her in Venice? How do you know it wasn't Holly Smith?"

Holly had filled him in with a very complete description of her cousin.

"Different woman. Same eyes. Shorter blond hair. But it was the eyes."

"And did you follow her?" It was subtle, but there was a shift in Mason's abrupt tone, a faint but discernible agitation.

"I lost her out of the station. When I spotted her it seemed beyond coincidental to me. Two women with those same incredible aquamarine eyes."

"You're sure about that?"

"Would I have missed the train to Budapest otherwise?" Gage was equally abrupt. Mason expected no less from him, and he didn't want to deviate from their standard exchange and tip his hand. Now for the non sequitur. "I did, however, pick her up later."

"Why the hell didn't you say so earlier?"

"I'm giving a sequential report."

"What address did you follow her to?"

Gage relayed the address where Holly'd been instructed to leave the package.

"Give me the address again and I'll run it." Mason's voice came across stone cold.

And now, for the coup de grâce... "She met two male subjects there. They were, shall we say, very friendly."

"'Very friendly' encompasses a wide range of behavior. Could you be more specific?"

"She was performing fellatio on one chap while the other one banged her from behind. Also, the female had a birthmark, more dark brown than red, roughly the size of a quid on her left buttock."

"Noted." Gage wagered there was red-hot heat behind the frost in Mason's voice.

"This morning at precisely 9:37 Holly Smith arrived at the address, left a package and continued to the airport."

"It took you nearly an hour to contact me with this?"

"I had to arrange a mobile. Shall I continue to monitor the female at that address or shall I go on to Budapest?"

"Proceed to Budapest as planned." Mason ended the call without a by-your-leave.

Gage turned to Holly, who sat wide-eyed on the edge of the bed. "Excellent. The fly's in the ointment. That was absolutely priceless inside information about the birthmark, luv."

Holly shook her head at the story Gage had concocted. "You think he'll contact her?"

"It's simply a matter of how quickly he can punch in the numbers." The device monitoring the bleed beeped. "There it is." He put it on speaker so Holly could hear, as well. "Show time."

"Hello?"

Holly nodded. "That's Josephine."

"How's my favorite monster today?" Mason asked, his voice silky smooth.

"Something's wrong. She should've delivered it by now, the stupid little bitch. I called her and reminded her again last night. I told her to take a water taxi and I'd cover the cost. But the GPS on her phone shows she's still at the hotel. She should've left an hour ago. Our buyer is getting very nervous and impatient. If she doesn't show up soon, the deal's off."

"Come, pet, it's unlike you to fret. A shame we don't have someone in place to check on her."

"No. It was too risky to involve anyone else."

"Where are you?" Mason asked.

"Where do you think I am? I'm at home, waiting. As soon as the money's wired into the account, I'm leaving for the airport."

"Are you sure your little cousin didn't deliver the package?"

"Of course I'm sure. My client would've been calling for the code instead of asking where the package is. The information's useless without the code and they don't get the code until we get the money."

"You wouldn't double-cross me on this, would you, pet?"

"We're already late delivering the package. I don't need you asking me something stupid like that on top of it."

"You lying whore." Mason exploded on the line and Holly jumped. "I have confirmation the package was delivered at 9:27." He recovered his aplomb. "If you want to fuck around in a threesome, have a go, but I want my bloody half of the money, you double-crossing bitch."

"What did you just say?"

"Which part is confusing for you, pet? That the bloody fucking package was delivered? That you were seen giving a blow job and being fucked at that address? That you're a lying whore, or that I want my half of the sodding money? I should've known better than to trust a woman."

Panic edged out the disdain in her voice. "You're a fool. You've been played."

"You may have played me for now, but I'll find you and when I do—"

"Not me, you idiot. Get off this phone and if you have a brain cell left, you'll get out of wherever you are right now." There was a distinctive click and the line went dead.

Holly's eyes were huge.

They'd played Mason like the mistrusting misogynist Gage had taken him for and Mason had ran true to form.

"I believe, luv, Mason just screwed the proverbial pooch."

"AND THAT'S IT?" HOLLY ASKED. She didn't know what she'd expected but it hadn't been this. Almost immediately after Mason hung up with Josephine, Gage had been contacted by both the CIA and Mason's superior, who'd secured Gage's number from his incoming call to Mason. Apparently they'd been suspicious and had been monitoring Mason. Gage had given them precisely the information they needed to prosecute him.

Josephine had been apprehended at home, Mason on his way out of his office. Both had sung like birds on the other, each bargaining information for lighter sentences.

"Aside from some potential briefing and questions, it's done. All governments involved would prefer this stay quiet." Gage set aside the phone and settled next to her on the bed.

Holly had expected agents to swarm them, take statements, escort them home. Instead everything had been conducted via phone with the recommendation that her family keep it quiet. Apparently clandestine meant clandestine in every respect. And then there was the tidbit that both assassination contracts had been canceled. One thing still niggled at her.

"How will we know she's being treated fairly? They could kill her."

"Holly, trust me on this. If you take it public, they'll be forced to make an example of her. If you allow it to unfold this way, it'll be much better for her. You do realize she'd hired an assassin to terminate you?"

Granted, they'd never been close, but the fact Josephine had actually planned her murder lanced her. Regardless, blood still bound them. "Yes. I just want to know she's going to get the help she so obviously needs." She raised her chin.

"I promise I'll see to it."

"Thank you." She'd known him only five short days, but she could trust that he was a man of his word. He had the connections. He'd take care of it.

"And now, luv, let's talk about us." He tugged her onto his lap. "Let's bump your flight out of London. A day's hardly enough time, but I can show you the gallery and my flat, introduce you to the inestimable Agnes, who will adore you because I do," he said with almost boyish enthusiasm.

Holly felt like a deer caught in headlights. Trapped and panicked. Was she in love with him? Of course. Who wouldn't be? He was this superhero kind of guy, larger than life. He was an extraordinary man. And she was just an ordinary, really very practical woman. Their worlds were vastly different. God, it was her mother and father all over again. Beautiful, worldly sophisticate hooks up with ordinary, off-the-farm realist. The magic was intense but it couldn't last. She'd lived with a lifetime of proof.

She wiggled off of his lap and stood, wrapping her arms around her middle. "I can't just bump my flight and hang out with you in London. I have a job to show up for on Monday morning, Gage. I'll be exhausted if I get in Sunday evening."

His enthusiasm definitely waned somewhat. "Fair enough. I have the more flexible schedule. If the plane's not full, and I doubt it is, I can go to Atlanta with you. I was supposed to be in Budapest next week, anyway. At least no one will be waiting to kill me in Atlanta."

"How can you joke about something like that?"

"I guess you didn't see the humor."

Really, all she could see was her mother telling her how miserable she'd been on the farm. The woman Holly had been before would've followed his lead and let him dictate a relationship that was destined to fail. Thank God, she wasn't that woman now. She could sit back and watch them destroy what they'd had or she could end it now and salvage a memory. She would not follow in her parents' footsteps.

"Gage…" How could she say this? How could she make him understand? "We've been on a wild, romantic ride. I know you think you love me and I love you, too. But now things are back to normal, and I really think it's best if we just chalk this up to a holiday romance."

"A holiday romance?" A frown knitted his heavy eyebrows.

"I've got a great story to tell my grandchildren one day." She smiled. "The spring I met an honest-to-goodness international spy when I went searching for my continental mother."

He stood and slowly approached her. "I agree. It will

make for a fascinating family story." He slid his hands over her shoulders and down her arms in a tingling caress. "But I want those grandchildren to be mine, as well." The wicked curl of his mouth set her pulse racing. "And I'm going to insist you heavily edit our dinner date and our gondola ride in the recounting. Wouldn't want to shock the kiddies."

She stepped away from him and slowly shook her head. She couldn't think clearly when he touched her, smiled at her that way. She didn't want her children to have the childhood she'd had, and quite frankly, she didn't see how the outcome could be any different. "I just don't see it happening."

This time, he was the one who nodded slowly. "After my parents died and it became apparent that the Colonel wished I'd not been a bloody nuisance and had had the common decency to die along with them, I never felt close to anyone. It wasn't a choice. It just was. There was a disconnect inside me. I liked people well enough, but no one mattered. I'm certain that was why I was recruited. It's a trait that serves one well as an operative. And then I met you." He shook his head slightly, as if he remained dazed by the encounter. "You were supposed to be the enemy. The bad guy. Of all the women I'd ever met, why did I feel connected to you? I spend most of my time observing people, art, life—one step removed. But with you, the buffer was gone. No matter how hard I tried to maintain that distance, I couldn't. I've faced life-and-death situations before and never told a woman I loved her. I meant what I said last night. You own those three words and there'll never be another woman who does."

She blinked away the tears stirred by his words. "I think we have fallen in love. That wonderful kind of love you experience when you're in a magical place and the day-to-day mundaneness of life doesn't intrude." She reached out to touch him but dropped her hand back to her side. "It's easy to be in love in Venice, Gage. Let's just savor it for what it was and not try to make it something it can't be."

"You want to put it on a shelf and take it out on cold lonely nights to admire it, is that it, Holly?"

She heard him. She also heard her father, his voice breaking, telling her he and her mother weren't the same kind of people. She loved Gage, but they weren't the same kind of people.

"You're an international spy—"

"*Was,* luv. Game up."

She ignored the interruption. "—who travels world-wide and has an art gallery in London. Can you really see yourself jumping up and down on the sidelines of a Little League game cheering as your son or daughter steals home? That's what I want, Gage. A nice, ordinary man to go with average, ordinary me." All those years, all she'd ever wanted was a nice, ordinary mother, not one who was larger than life, one who was never there for her. And she certainly didn't want a larger-than-life husband.

"You won't even give us a chance, will you?"

She shook her head. "It's better this way." Straightening her spine, she added, "I have a plane to catch."

"I'll have your bags packed and sent to you," he said with a curt nod.

Holly breathed an inward sigh of relief. He'd let it go, thank God. "That's not necessary."

"It's a minor detail in the clean-up. Shall we ship them to your house or would you prefer to claim them at the airport?" He was pleasantly efficient, but she could sense the hurt roiling inside him. Perhaps not today, but one day he'd thank her for this. At least he wasn't being a bastard about it.

"If you're going to take care of it, my house, please." She gave him the information. It wasn't as if he couldn't find her address if he wanted it, anyway.

"Very good. Now, let's get you to your plane." He placed his hand in the small of her back, ushering her toward the door, his touch burning through her clothes.

She stopped and looked at him, at the classic profile, the slightly overlong hair lapping at his collar. "You don't have to do this, Gage."

"Nonsense. With your abysmal sense of direction, you might never make it to the airport. I'll see you to the terminal." He opened the door of the squalid little room and bowed for her to go out ahead of him.

Gallant to the end.

Holly stepped out into blinding sunlight and the harsh realities of the Mestre. Across the lagoon lay a world of magic and enchantment, but it was a world removed.

She was right. She knew she was right. She'd lived a lifetime with a man who'd made a similar mistake and seen the consequences firsthand.

Why, then, did she feel like throwing up?

16

"I'M WORRIED ABOUT MING," Holly said to her stepmother, as Marcia passed her a glass of iced tea.

Everything else had settled into a rhythm. Her family had moved through shock and grief and forgiveness at Josephine's betrayal to the point that Holly's dad had visited her last week at a psychiatric prison facility where she was getting the help they all wanted for her. Whether she would ever walk the streets as a free woman again, however, was doubtful. Nobody expected any less for crimes of treason.

Everything was back to normal. Except Ming.

It had been two months and he wouldn't eat, wouldn't play, wouldn't do anything but lie around curled up in a ball. He wouldn't even lie on her lap.

Catnip? He could care less.

The ball in the wheel he'd always loved? Forget it.

She'd taken him to the vet, who'd run a barrage of tests costing a small fortune only to pronounce him physically fine.

She, on the other hand, was eating for both of them. If it wasn't tied down or didn't fight back, it was fair game. She was eating every bloody thing in sight. And the bloody word *bloody* had become a routine part of her stream of consciousness regardless of how bloody hard she tried to cull it.

"Are you going to eat those fries?" she asked Marcia. She'd made home fries and coleslaw to go with their hot dogs for their once-a-month mother-stepdaughter get-together at Holly's house.

Marcia cupped a protective hand around her plate and looked at Holly. "I think so."

Sheesh. She'd just asked. Seemed a shame to waste a good home fry. "Oh. Okay."

"You're not…you know…"

"What?"

"Any chance you're pregnant?"

"No." They'd been careful and she'd had her period since then.

"Well, you've just been different ever since you got back from Venice. You've got a different energy field."

"Thank you." She dredged her fry through ketchup. "I went to Venice to be different. That was the point."

"I'm thinking the point wasn't to gain seven pounds and sit around unhappy." Marcia could be blunt.

"I told you I'm worried about Ming."

"Whatever you say. Got any big plans for the summer? The kids are out already. When do you finish up?"

"Next week. I'm thinking I'll paint the kitchen and clean out a couple of closets."

Marcia clapped her hands in faux enthusiasm. "Ooh. Watching paint dry. Be sure and invite me over."

Holly laughed. "We'll see if I get around to it."

"Charles and I sort of thought you might've caught the travel bug with your trip to Venice this spring." Marcia fiddled with her fork. "You did enjoy it, didn't you? Well, other than almost being killed by your cousin and getting embroiled in an international ring of double-crossing spies? Well, and finding out your mother is a total bitch?" Marcia had the most amazing capacity for conversation.

"Other than those little blips on the radar, it was fabulous."

"I thought so." She offered Holly a big smile. "And that's such a great hairstyle you came back with. I'm glad you decided to keep your hair short like that. It suits you. It's very fashionable."

That was pretty much what her female students had told her—and Brett Brown, whom she was fairly certain had a bit of a crush on her. She told Marcia the same thing she'd told them. "It's not fashionable. I'm not a fashionable kind of woman." The whole fashionable issue got her back up.

"Holly. Stop." Marcia reached across the table and placed her hand over Holly's. "Honey, stop trying so hard not to be like her. I know I'm just the stepmother here, and I'm sure I'm crossing all kinds of boundaries, but I've got to speak my piece. Good, bad or indifferent, she's your mother and there's some genetic transference. Being fashionable isn't a crime, honey, and it doesn't make you like her. You can be fashionable and ambitious and have dreams and be part of a world that's bigger than where you are now and it doesn't make you Julia. It also doesn't make you disloyal to your father." She squeezed Holly's hand and then released her.

Marcia wouldn't be so bloody gracious about Julia if she knew how Holly's father still felt. "I know he still loves her," Marcia continued. Well, maybe she wouldn't be bent out of shape. "And I know he loves me, too. If she ever shows up, I'm not sure how well I'll fare, but for now, I'm the one he comes home to every day. I'm the one who gets a back rub at night and a goodbye kiss every morning."

Holly pushed away from the table and cleared their plates. "How do you stand it? Knowing part of him still loves her?"

"Because love and life are imperfect and you've got to seize your chance at happiness whenever you can."

Holly placed a slice of apple pie in front of each of them and sat back down. "He's lucky to have you."

"He is, isn't he? And I'm lucky to have him." Marcia cut into her pie. "And speaking of love, Kyle told your daddy Tom Brandtly asked for your phone number."

Tom was her nephew Jeremy's Little League coach. Divorced with a son Jeremy's age, Tom owned a real estate company. He'd seen Holly at Jeremy's game and asked Kyle about her. The guy seemed nice. No shivers ran down her spine at the sound of his voice, but then, most men's voices didn't set her aquiver. Actually, only one man's voice did that and he wasn't in the running. She'd crossed him off the list two months ago. "He called last week. We've talked on the phone a couple of times."

"And?" Marcia forked in a bite of pie "Um, delicious. You make the best apple pie."

"Thanks. Take the rest home for you and Daddy." If it stayed here she'd just eat it—before she went to bed. Alone.

"Will do." She scooped up another mouthful. "And what about Tom?"

"I don't know." Holly shrugged.

"What's not to know? He's a good-looking guy with a

good job, nice house and his kid isn't a smart aleck. He sort of reminds me a little of a young Robert Redford. Has he asked you out?"

With sandy hair, blue eyes and a nice square jaw, he *was* a good-looking guy, even though Holly thought comparing him to a young Redford was a stretch. But then again, Marcia thought her dad looked like Jeremy Irons in overalls and that was just…well, out there. Regardless, Tom did jump and scream and cheer his kid into home— well, he actually did that for everyone's kid. He was, after all, a Little League coach with all-American blond good looks. A nice, average, ordinary guy had been dropped in her lap. "He invited me to the Little League barbecue as his date."

"You said yes, didn't you?"

"I told him I'd let him know." What was wrong with her that she hadn't accepted immediately?

Because the idea of his hand on her arm or around her waist made her cringe? Because the thought of a good-night kiss made her queasy? Because he wasn't Gage Bloody Retired International Spy and Art Gallery Owner Carswell, that's why she'd told him she'd let him bloody well know.

He was a nice guy, but she wasn't sure if he even knew where Prague was. And she was almost a hundred percent sure he wouldn't rise from the table when she excused herself to go to the ladies' room. He wouldn't sing Italian operas in the shower and he wouldn't dare to bring her back-to-back orgasms in a gondola. He wasn't a goddamned larger-than-life superhero who would bring her a cold cloth and blot her eyes when she'd fallen to pieces.

Quite simply, he wasn't Gage.

"Well, I've got a suggestion," Marcia said. "I think you should contact this pet psychic."

Holly stopped, her fork halfway to her mouth. "What?"

"You said you were worried about Ming." Yeah, like ten minutes ago, but that was the way a conversation with Marcia often went, it skipped all over the place. "I've got the name of a pet psychic because we've been having problems with Gidget."

"You're kidding, right? A pet psychic?"

"It couldn't hurt. Didn't you say the vet couldn't find anything wrong with him?"

"Well, yeah, but… How much does it cost?"

"Sixty-five dollars for half an hour."

Holly nearly choked. Sixty-five dollars? Marcia had to be kidding. Ming raised his head and slanted her an accusatory look from his bright blue eyes. She had to do something for him. She couldn't just sit by while he wasted away. "Fine. Give me her number. I'll call."

Marcia smiled and patted Holly's hand across the table. "The things we do for love."

"YOU'RE DRIVING US ALL MAD. Would you just pick up the sodding phone and ring her?" Agnes demanded, standing in front of his desk all cross and fussy.

"Bloody good thing you possess outstanding organizational skills or I wouldn't put up with your cheek," Gage retorted. They both knew she ran the gallery flawlessly and that he'd lop off his right hand before he let her go. "She doesn't want me to ring her."

"How do you know?"

"She said."

"She's a woman. We never say what we mean."

He leaned back in his chair and crossed his arms over his chest. "I'm not stalking her, Agnes."

"I didn't suggest you stalk her, Gage. I suggested ringing her. There's a vast difference between a 'hello, how are you?' and sitting outside her flat with night-vision goggles."

"She knows how I feel about her."

"Maybe I should call her. Someone has to straighten out this bleeding mess the two of you are making."

"Not even your formidable organizational skills at running this gallery would save your post if you called her."

Agnes snorted in disgust. "I didn't say I was. I simply said I should. If something doesn't happen we're all going to drop dead of exhaustion."

"Complaining about your wages and work now?"

"No need to be a prick."

Gage scrubbed his hand through his hair. He supposed he had been somewhat…driven. The agency had offered him Mason's position as a handler. He'd promptly declined. That'd drive him nutters in no time. He'd known the day he got off the Budapest-bound train that his time with the agency was done. And it was. But now he had too much time on his hands.

He'd thought if he worked hard enough, he wouldn't miss Holly so desperately, wouldn't ache for her touch, for the sweet melody of her voice, for her scent, for the taste of her mouth. So far that hadn't happened. But he was well on his way to having a new gallery in Prague.

"I don't understand you. You aren't going to forget her this way," Agnes said, shaking her head and indicating the painting of Holly dominating the wall opposite his desk.

He looked at it again, for perhaps the hundredth time that morning. He'd commissioned it from one of the camera stills he'd taken. He'd reviewed hours of footage to find precisely what he wanted. It was the evening of their gondola ride and she'd been preparing to go out. Her hair was pinned up and she'd been in the process of shrugging out of the robe. It had nearly slipped off, caught in the crook of her elbows, the back open to her buttocks, leaving the elegant line of her neck, shoulders and back bare. She'd chosen that moment to glance over her shoulder. Breathtakingly sensual and erotic. His Holly.

He looked at Agnes. She simply didn't get it. "The point's never been to forget her. That's impossible. I simply want her to be happy."

"Well, then, maybe you shouldn't be so quick to settle back on your arse and do nothing."

"MING IS VERY UNHAPPY," Delores, the pet psychic, announced over the phone.

Well, thank God. She'd parted with sixty-five dollars to discern that. Hel-lo. And how could the woman know anything over the phone? Still, she knew Ming was unhappy. "Uh, can you get him to tell you why?"

"He says he loves you but he loves another better." There was a pause on the other end of the line. "Do you know a Gigi…wait…Gidgie…"

"Gidget?"

"Yes. That's it. Gidget. Ming is pining for Gidget. Do you know this Gidget?"

"It's my stepmother's toy poodle. Gidget's a dog."

"Ming says, 'Correction.' Gidget's his bitch."

"But he's a cat and she's a dog." They weren't even the same kind. Ming shot her a baleful look from the sofa. "Sorry. She's his bitch." She kneeled down in front of Ming. "What if I get you a nice girl kitty? We could check with the rescue group for a girl Siamese."

Ming hissed and Holly stood up and backed away. Okay, Delores didn't need to psychically interpret that. Nonetheless, she did. "Ming says he doesn't want an insipid—"

"He actually used that word?"

"Yes." Wow. Her cat had quite the vocabulary. "He doesn't want an insipid Siamese feline."

"But why?"

Did he just roll his eyes?

"He says what part of this don't you understand? He wants Gidget. Only she will do."

Okay. A smart-ass with a good vocabulary.

"Fine. I'll call Marcia and arrange to take him out tomorrow."

"Not just for a visit. He wants to stay."

"Okay." Now she was losing her cat.

"I'm throwing this in for free. You should go."

"I already said I'll take him tomorrow."

"No. A man waits for you. You should follow your heart and go to him."

Please. She couldn't believe she was going to ask this, but it was a moment of weakness and she'd been so thoroughly miserable. "If I go to him, will it last?"

"He's the one. But whether it lasts, well, that's up to the two of you."

"Thank you."

"One other thing."

"Yes?"

"Ming says now that he's finally got your attention, could he have some canned tuna? He's starving."

17

"EXCUSE ME. I'M LOOKING FOR Gage Carswell." She was so nervous. Don't throw up. Don't throw up. Tossing her breakfast wasn't good at any time, but it'd be especially bad to do it on the gleaming wooden floors in the elegant salon in what was a much nicer section of London than some. On her trip from the airport, she'd mostly found London to be hot and dirty. It was no Venice.

"Do you have an appoint—" The receptionist looked up and her eyes widened, as if she recognized her, but Holly'd never laid eyes on the cool blonde before. "Oh, yes, quite. Up those stairs, left down the hall, first door on the right. Agnes will be delighted to assist you, ma'am." Good grief. She wouldn't have been surprised if the receptionist had bowed. The woman had obviously mistaken her for someone else. But if it got her in to see Gage, she'd roll with it.

Holly's knees shook so badly, she could hardly climb the stairs.

She followed the directions and walked through a red lacquered door. A gorgeous woman, late twenties, possibly early thirties, who looked more as if she belonged on a runway than in an art gallery, sat in front of a computer. Porcelain-white skin, jet-black hair cut in an abbreviated bob, black glasses, which would've looked frumpy on Holly but were chic and sophisticated on this creature, perched on the end of a flawless nose, all cut an intimidating figure.

"Excuse me, please. I'm looking for Agnes."

"I'm Agnes." The woman looked up and did a double-take. She stood. Immediately, Holly felt every ounce of the seven pounds she'd gained. Agnes must've been five eleven, maybe six feet, all of a size two…and a paragon of administrative genius to boot, according to Gage. Holly struggled not to hate her on sight. "And you are Holly Smith." She extended a long, thin hand and Holly automatically reached out and shook it. "Thank goodness! I thought you'd never get here."

Panic fluttered in her chest. "What do you mean? Did someone try to contact me? Has something happened to Gage?" God, no. She'd wasted all this time. Nothing could happen to him. After all, nothing happened to larger-than-life superheroes.

Agnes looked at her as if she'd lost her mind. "He's fine. Ridiculously high-minded if you ask me, but fine, nonetheless. He'd be buggered if he'd call you. Blathered on about how he only wanted you to be happy."

"He said that?" She managed not to gape in front of the gorgeous Agnes, but it was a close call.

"Is this news to you? He assured me you knew how he felt. I'm going to kill him if he didn't tell you when he said he did."

"Well, he did, but…he told you?"

Agnes rolled her eyes. "It's not as if he hasn't told everyone." Agnes stepped out from behind the desk. "Come with me."

Holly followed the beautiful Agnes into another room, immaculate and sleekly appointed with a blend of wood and leather and glass.

"As I said, how he feels is no secret." She pointed to a wall opposite the glass and near-black wood desk. Holly's world tilted on its axis.

"That's me."

"God save the queen and the rest of us from idiots and lovers." Holly wasn't about to ask the very intimidating Agnes whether she fell into the idiot or lover category. "He's buggy for you, you know. Wouldn't call in case you thought he was stalking you. Finally had me order a book on Little League rules." She wrinkled her nose. "I'm assuming that was on your behalf."

"I'm pretty sure." Holly looked around. "Where is he?"

"The two of you are absolutely killing me. He's in Prague."

"He's in Prague?"

Agnes sighed as if she were Atlas bearing the weight of an ungrateful world. "I'll arrange your travel—"

"That's not necessary."

"Of course it is. Otherwise I'll encounter a lynch mob with the staff. With you there, we expect he'll have something to do rather than work us all to death. How soon would you like to arrive?"

"Now."

Another sigh. "That's what I thought. If wishes were horses…" Agnes was beginning to grow on her.

THE BELL OVER THE FRONT door sounded as he stood at the roughed-in reception area reviewing the last-minute lighting changes. Finally. It was bloody inconvenient that

Agnes had asked him to sign for a delivery this morning. Didn't he pay wages for staff to handle things like that?

He waved to the far side of the wall. "Place it over there. And I presume I need to sign for it."

Silence.

He glanced up.

Holly. He closed his eyes. He'd suspected he was going mad, now he knew for sure. He was seeing Holly in lieu of the brown-uniformed chap.

He opened his eyes. She was still there. Obviously he'd gone stark raving nutters.

"Gage—"

Now he was imagining her soft, honeyed voice. "Luv? Are you here or have I truly lost my mind?"

He *felt* her joy, her relief, and he *knew* it was her, knew she was really here in Prague.

Within seconds he had her in his arms. Flesh and blood. Real. He buried his fingers in her hair, against her scalp, cupped her head in his hands, slanted his mouth over hers and kissed her with all the longing and hunger he'd felt for the past two-and-a-half months. She answered him with a craving and need that matched his own.

Gage walked her backward until she stood sandwiched between the wall and him. She reached between them and cupped his cock in her hand, her fingers molding his already-rigid penis through his trousers.

"My flat…upstairs…there's a bed…."

"No. Here. Now." Her eyes glittered with that light he knew so well. They were in the lobby. While no one else was around, the front door was unlocked and the window was just to his left. But his sweet little near-exhibitionist was already unzipping him.

He lifted the hem of her dress and pulled aside the crotch of her knickers to find her plump nether lips pouting a wet invitation. She delved inside his trousers and he groaned aloud when she wrapped her hand around his shaft. She wrapped her other arm around his neck, pulling his head back down to hers, her mouth latching on to his, her tongue beckoning an invitation.

He released her knickers long enough to lift her leg to his hip, opening her. He tugged the material aside again, his knuckles grazing her curls and her honey-slicked entrance. She uttered a soft whimpering noise into his mouth and guided his cock to her slick channel. One thrust and he was in her, surrounded by tight wet silk. Her mouth was equally hot and wet, her tongue intertwined with his.

He claimed her. *Mine.* She answered him, grinding against him. *Yours.*

He pistoned into her, hard and fast. *Mine. Mine. Mine.* She tightened her muscles around his cock as the first wave of her orgasm rocked through her. It felt so bloody good to shout her name as he came inside her.

His cock was still buried deep, small tremors running through him when she nuzzled his jaw. "Does that mean you're glad to see me?"

"You're looking well," Gage said as she walked out of the bathroom upstairs in his apartment at the top of the gallery.

"Thank you. So are you." He looked beyond well, even though he seemed a bit haggard, as if he hadn't been sleeping well. And she was pretty sure he'd dropped a few pounds, which he hadn't needed to drop in the first place. Patently unfair—she'd gained weight and he'd lost.

The room was small but sumptuous—a melding of East meets West, resplendent with exotic fabrics and exquisite furniture. "You didn't tell me you were sinfully rich."

Gage shrugged. "It never came up. I didn't think it'd matter to you. Please, take a seat." He chose a single armchair upholstered in a richly patterned gold and burgundy, which left her to perch on the low-slung divan. "Quite a tidy sum from insurance policies went into trust when my parents died. And I was the Colonel's only heir." He offered another shrug. "I brought in a bit of income as an operative and the gallery's done rather well."

"You also didn't tell me you were minor royalty."

"Agnes?"

Holly nodded. Agnes had also mentioned that Gage was a generous benefactor to numerous charities and an employer who looked after his people very well. But Holly kept those tidbits to herself. It was as if Agnes felt she needed to make sure Holly never considered leaving.

"Some cheek she has, that one. I'm going to wind up sacking her yet. What was the point in telling you? It never came up, and it certainly wasn't going to further my cause, was it? It's not as if I'm taking tea with the queen." He skewed her with a speculative look from his dark eyes. "I'll wager you almost changed your mind about coming when you found out, didn't you?"

"The thought did cross my mind." For about a second. Until Agnes got one good look at her and informed her in no uncertain terms that Holly was going to Prague, even if the staff had to kidnap her and drive her across Europe in the firm's delivery truck themselves.

Gage grinned. "Agnes can be very persuasive."

"That's one way to put it. You never said she was young and gorgeous."

"I suppose she is. She's mostly bloody efficient. And I told you she would adore you."

"Adoration would be stretching it, but I think she liked me well enough."

"Booked your flight and had a car meet you at the airport in Prague, did she? I suppose I can't sack her yet."

"She also arranged my hotel room." She hadn't arrived expecting to stay with him.

He frowned. "Nearby, I trust."

She told him the name and he nodded approvingly. Finally all the chitchat was past and only the hard questions that wanted answers remained between them.

That last hour in Venice, he'd stepped out on a limb, bared his soul, handed her his heart, and she'd handed it back. She hoped he was more generous with her now that the tables were turned.

"I'm not exactly sure where to start." She twisted her hands together and he waited. "I love you."

"That's a most excellent place to start."

But he wasn't doing backflips, understandably so. They'd covered this ground in Venice.

"I've spent a lot of years with some screwy notions."

"Most of us have."

"Some of us more crazy than others. I…uh…quit my job. I've got my résumé ready and I've put out some preliminary feelers in London, Venice and here. I've had some interest, so I'm fairly certain I can find something. Agnes has commandeered the task of finding me an apartment."

"You don't need to work, you know," he said, tracing the chair's arm with his fingertip. She loved his hands.

She looked at him, challenging him. "Neither do you, but you do. I can't sit around all day, just being some rich man's girlfriend. I need to work and I'm good at what I do." He inclined his dark head in acknowledgment. "I want to give us a chance. I want this to work. But our relationship doesn't need the pressure of my having given up everything to follow you here. If, in three months, you discover you really can't live with some of my less-charming quirks, then I'll still have an apartment and a job and it won't be awkward for either one of us. It's the fairest chance we can give our relationship, that is, if you still want one."

"I still want one. And what happens when it's confirmed I absolutely can't live without all of your quirks, charming or otherwise?"

"We'll cross that bridge when we come to it." She had a good, good feeling about this, about them. "I understand you've been boning up on Little League plays."

"And practicing my cheering. How's this?" He unfolded himself from his chair and then suddenly began jumping up and down and yelled, "Run, Timmy, run. Slide into the little bugger if he doesn't get out of your bloody way." He stopped and flashed a wicked grin. "How'd I do, luv?"

Holly laughed. "I don't think you're supposed to encourage the children to hurt the other ones. And you'll have to watch the swearing."

"Ah. I'll work on it some more, then." He sobered and crossed to the divan, kneeling on one knee, pressing her back until she reclined and he lay beside her. "You know I was coming for you. I told you I'd stay away, but I couldn't." He stroked her hair back from her face, and the tenderness in that simple gesture nearly stole her breath. "I'd planned to come after this gallery opening."

She caught his hand and brought it to her mouth, pressing a kiss to the small scar on the back. "And what if I'd been involved with someone else?"

"Then that would've been that—if you'd been happy. If you weren't, I would've lobbied my case. Saved me a plane trip, you did. What changed your mind?" He twined his fingers through hers.

"A lot of things kept slapping me in the face, but I think it was Delores who finally pushed me over the edge." She explained about Ming's pining and her consulting Delores, the pet psychic.

"You, my tight-fisted little grubber, paid a pet psychic and then gave up your job—"

She tried to look down her nose at him, but it was nearly impossible flat on her back. "—and rented out my condo furnished."

"And came over here because a pet psychic told you to?" He was laughing at her.

"Well, she was right about Ming." Ming had perked right up when she took him out to her dad and Marcia's to be with Gidget, his own true doggie love. Following Delores's advice for herself had seemed extremely prudent at the time.

And then, everything seemed to fall into place, as if the universe had just been waiting on her to come to the correct conclusion. One of the student teachers at school had needed an apartment to rent for the upcoming school year. She'd been thrilled to rent Holly's place and Holly had been more than willing because Susanne shared Holly's germ "awareness."

Gage scattered nibbling kisses along her neck and a shiver danced through her. Had he even heard what she'd said about Ming? "Besides, I was running out of excuses to turn down Tom Brandtly."

He raised his head, frowning. "Who the bloody hell is Tom Brandtly?"

"My nephew's Little League coach." She smiled sweetly. "He kept asking me out."

"Bugger Tom Brandtly."

Holly laughed and drew his head back down to her. "Hmm. I'd much rather bugger you."

Epilogue

"OH MY GOD. YOU'RE ACTUALLY nervous about meeting my father, aren't you?" Funny how the more she traveled by plane, the less traumatic it was. And Gage, the seasoned traveler, had been a veritable wreck since they'd left Heathrow for Atlanta.

"I've been shagging his daughter all over Europe for the past seven months—bloody right I'm nervous."

Holly laughed.

"What's so bloody funny?" he growled.

"You. How many times have you faced down enemy agents and been calm, cool and collected, and now… My dad is a sweetie. Honest."

"Go ahead and laugh. It's not every day a bloke asks for a man's daughter's hand in marriage."

"I told you, you don't have to do that."

"And I told you I do."

Another one of his gallant notions. He had the ring. She knew it, but she hadn't seen it, although Agnes assured her she'd love it. She didn't doubt it for a second.

He'd dragged Agnes along to help him pick it out. Agnes, the closest thing to family Gage had, had become like a sister to Holly.

She and Gage had discussed marriage and children and

where they'd live, but he hadn't officially asked her to marry him. He'd insisted on meeting her family and asking her father first. In his eyes, that was the only right way to do it.

"So, you think he'll be okay with us living abroad until we start a family?"

That was loosely the plan. "I think when we start having children, he'll want to play the doting grandfather. But honestly, I think he just wants me to be happy whether I'm in Europe or Atlanta."

"And are you?"

Every day wasn't a picnic. She found it incredibly annoying that he couldn't manage to cap the toothpaste after he used it, and even though there was a little basket by the door for the mail, he left it scattered on the kitchen counter. On the other hand, he was incredibly tolerant of her quirks, which probably weren't so easy to live with. But the main thing she'd discovered was that while it was easy to be in love in Venice and a bit harder with the day-to-day routine of life, they were still in love, more so now than then.

"I am deliriously happy. And Daddy's going to be happy, too, when he figures out what I've learned."

"What's that, luv?"

"I've discovered that I'm in love with an extraordinary man who's ruined me for all others. Nobody does it better than you."

He leaned forward, relaxing, a wicked smile curling his lips. "Does what?"

"Why, everything."

* * * * *

BRIANNA STRETCHED OUT beside Ewan, languid as a cat, and promptly fell asleep. Midday sunshine streamed into the chamber, bathing her lovely, long-limbed body in golden light, the sea-scented breeze wafting inside to dry the damp red-gold tendrils curling about her flushed face. Propping himself up on one elbow, Ewan slid his gaze over her. She looked beautiful and whole, satisfied and sated, and altogether happier than he had so far seen her. A slight smile curved her beautiful lips as though she must be in the midst of a lovely dream. She'd molded her lush, lovely body to his and laid her head in the curve of his shoulder and settled in to sleep beside him. For the longest while he lay there turned toward her, content to watch her sleep, at near perfect peace.

Not wholly perfect, for she had yet to answer his marriage proposal. Still, she wanted to make a baby with him, and Ewan no longer viewed her plan as the travesty he once had. He wanted children—sons to carry on after him, though a bonny little daughter with flame-colored hair would be nice, too. But he also wanted more than to simply plant his seed and be on his way. He wanted to lie beside Brianna night upon night as she increased, rub soothing unguents into the swell of her belly, knead the ache from her back and make slow, gentle love to her. He wanted to hold his newly born child in his arms and look down into Brianna's tired but radiant face and blot the perspiration from her brow and be a husband to her in every way.

He gave her a gentle nudge. "Brie?"

"Hmm?"

She rolled onto her side and he captured her against his chest. One arm wrapped about her waist, he bent to her ear and asked, "Do you think we might have just made a baby?"

Her eyes remained closed, but he felt her tense against him. "I don't know. We'll have to wait and see."

He stroked his hand over the flat plane of her belly. "You're so small and tight it's hard to imagine you increasing."

"All women increase no matter how large or small they start out. I may not grow big as a croft, but I'll be big enough, though I have hopes I may not waddle like a duck, at least not too badly."

The reference to his fair-day teasing was not lost on him. He grinned. "Brianna MacLeod grown so large she must sit still for once in her life. I'll need the proof of my own eyes to believe it."

Despite their banter, he felt his spirits dip. Assuming they were so blessed, he wouldn't have the chance to see her thus. By then he would be long gone, restored to his clan according to the sad bargain they'd struck. He opened his mouth to ask her to marry him again and then clamped it closed, not wanting to spoil the moment, but the unspoken words weighed like a millstone on his heart.

The damnable bargain they'd struck was proving to be a devil's pact indeed.

* * * * *

Will these two star-crossed lovers
find their sexily-ever-after?
Find out in
BOUND TO PLEASE
by Hope Tarr,
available in July wherever
Harlequin® Blaze™ books are sold.

HARLEQUIN® *Blaze*

Harlequin Blaze marks new territory with its first historical novel!

For years readers have trusted the Harlequin Blaze series to entertain them with a variety of stories— Now Blaze is breaking down the final barrier— the time barrier!

Welcome to Blaze Historicals—all the sexiness you love in a Blaze novel, all the adventure of a historical romance. It's the best of both worlds!

Don't miss the first book in this exciting new miniseries:

BOUND TO PLEASE
by **Hope Tarr**

New laird Brianna MacLeod knows she can't protect her land or her people without a man by her side. So what else can she do—she kidnaps one! Only, she doesn't expect to find herself the one enslaved....

Available in July wherever Harlequin books are sold.

▼ *Silhouette*®

SPECIAL EDITION™

NEW YORK TIMES BESTSELLING AUTHOR

DIANA PALMER

A brand-new Long, Tall Texans novel

HEART OF STONE

Feeling unwanted and unloved, Keely returns to Jacobsville and to Boone Sinclair, a rancher troubled by his own past. Boone has always seemed reserved, but now Keely discovers a sensuality with him that quickly turns to love. Can they each see past their own scars to let love in?

*Available September 2008
wherever you buy books.*

HIGH-SOCIETY SECRET PREGNANCY

Park Avenue Scandals

Self-made millionaire Max Rolland had given
up on love until he meets socialite fundraiser
Julia Prentice. After their encounter Julia finds
herself pregnant, but a mysterious blackmailer
threatens to use this surprise pregnancy and ruin
his reputation. Max must decide whether to turn
his back on the woman carrying his child or risk
everything, including his heart....

**Don't miss the next installment of
the Park Avenue Scandals series—
Front Page Engagement
by Laura Wright—
coming in August 2008
from Silhouette Desire!**

Always Powerful, Passionate and Provocative.

SPECIAL EDITION™

Little did hotel-chain CFO Tom Holloway
realize that his new executive assistant
spelled trouble. But even though
single mom Shelly Winston was planted
by Holloway's worst enemy to take him
down, Shelly was no dupe—she had
a mind of her own and an eye for
her handsome boss.

Look for

IN BED
WITH THE BOSS

by *USA TODAY* bestselling author
CHRISTINE RIMMER

*Available July
wherever you buy books.*

REQUEST YOUR FREE BOOKS!

2 FREE NOVELS
PLUS 2
FREE GIFTS!

HARLEQUIN®

Blaze ™

Red-hot reads!

HB08R